Thelma and the Whore of Babylon

By
Fritz Damler

https://www.facebook.com/pages/Fritz-
Damler/388247417952821?ref=hl

Many thanks to Seth Taylor, for his cover illustrations and Mari
Anderson, for her patient editing and cover design,

Chapter 1

The scent of gardenias teased Thelma from her afternoon nap. It made her wrinkle her nose, shift uneasily against the sternpost and scratch at a persistent tickle on her bum. The cloying smell overpowered the comforting odor of her bilge water and interrupted a nostalgic dream of wallowing in Maldon River mud. She blew a wispy lock of graying hair from her face and popped open one eye. It took her a moment to focus in the gloom, but there was no mistaking she wasn't alone. *Oh my, another lost soul.*

There had been a rash of them lately. What with the testy economy and all, people were selling off their boats as if they were a bad curse. But it was some that bought 'em caused all the trouble. Imagine, changing the name of a vessel with no respect for its original soul. Heavens, where did those people think the old name went? Seems the displaced dears were everywhere these days looking for a nameless hull to claim as their own.

This young thing was certainly the prettiest one she'd seen. An iridescent sheen glowed from the woman's shoulder length black hair. It made the white gown she wore look almost regal. Thelma envied the woman's full red lips and delicate features, but she was put off by the deep indigo eyes that never seemed to blink. Oddly enough, her ghostly translucence seemed less pronounced than most, as though she had a wee bit of substance.

Thelma sat up, cleared her throat and patted at the tight row of curlers in her hair. She always took pity on the homeless. "A shame ain't it, luv? Well, you've come to the right place. I'll fix ya' a nice cuppa tea and butter a few scones."

The young woman arched her eyebrows and tucked in her chin. "I beg your pardon?" She had the voice of a nightclub singer–that deep, almost raspy quality, but with a haughty edge. She placed her hands on her hips with a flash of crimson nails. "I want nothing from you, and I'll give you ten minutes to clear out."

Thelma clutched her worn, daisy print terrycloth robe to her throat. It stretched a bit, but she'd been built broad of beam. "A bit touchy ain't we, luv? You have nothing to fear from me. I'll help you find a new home."

"It's you that needs a new home, granny. In case you hadn't noticed, this is my place now."

Thelma had a fair amount of tolerance for the displaced, but this one had gone too far. *The cheek, coming aboard uninvited and ordering me about–and that perfume!* She sniffed and tossed her head. "See here, Missy, that kind of talk will get you nowhere. A civil tongue is what you need. Mind you, it might seem the end of the world now, but the weather always changes for the better after a storm."

The young woman stooped, dug into a black satchel at her side and pulled out a gold-framed hand-mirror with an ivory handle. She gave herself a once over, tucking in a loose strand of black hair. "You'd better hope for your sake the weather is better, 'cause you're outta here." The woman lowered her mirror and gave an impudent thrust of her chin. "Have a look."

"What's this nonsense?" Thelma began, but her voice died when she looked over her shoulder. She gaped at her oak transom, the fresh coat of paint and the horrifying sight of an old geezer printing a new name. The stylish Gothic lettering read THEODO. His brush was poised to add another letter. *Good heavens, that must have been the tickle on my bum.*

Thelma's name was gone. She'd been painted out as though she were never there. "But, but," she sputtered. "There's been some mistake. I'm not for sale. Why, my owner was just here yesterday giving us a wash."

The woman held the mirror to Thelma's face. "Take a good look dearie, in a few minutes you'll be gone for good."

"I'd have known," Thelma said, her voice shrill with panic. "There're no secrets aboard. Only a week ago I heard him planning another cruise."

"There's another cruise planned all right," said the woman, "but with a new owner and it's me he'll be sailing."

Thelma fought for breath. She felt faint and for the first time in her life she felt...good God, seasick. She reached out and steadied herself on one of her heavy oak frames. *This can't be. But it would explain the opaque quality of this youngster. She seems to flesh out with each new letter on my transom.* Thelma held her hand to a spray of light flooding through a porthole. *Good Lord! I can see through my hand. Can it be true? I can't possibly leave my home.*

I'm nearly eighty years old. I wouldn't live a day without my old timbers to keep me afloat. She took a slow breath, trying to collect her wits and muster a shred of dignity. "So, then you'll be?"

"Theodora Regina. Queen Theodora to you, honey."

At that moment Thelma sensed the familiar list as her owner, a retired colonel in his seventies, stepped aboard. She pointed a gnarly finger at the queen. "Now we'll get to the bottom of this, Missy."

A young man followed the colonel over Thelma's bulwarks; her fir decks barely noticed the extra weight. She recognized him from a few weeks ago—tall, muscular, with wavy brown hair that would have passed muster in Lord Nelson's day. The colonel had shown him around her hull, giving the same little tour he willingly gave any curious dock-walker. She recalled now that this particular young man had been full of questions about her sailing qualities and seaworthiness and had listened eagerly to the colonel's favorite sea yarns.

"I believe you'll find everything shipshape. She's a well-found vessel, known where I'm from as an old English lead mine. Displaces fifteen tons, a considerable amount for thirty-five feet, but able to handle any sea you might encounter. A bit temperamental under power, have to watch the gauges, belt slips and she overheats. See that you watch your step on the bowsprit; they don't call them 'widow makers' for nothing. She's carried me over fifty thousand miles and you couldn't ask for a more forgiving helm.

The young man gave one of Thelma's sheet winches a spin. "I knew the minute I saw her she was the boat for me. They just don't make 'em like this anymore." His gaze drifted up the spruce mast. "I'm still surprised you agreed to sell her."

The colonel stood in the cockpit and rested one arm on the boom. "Son, the old gal needs a fair bit of muscle to sail her and that's something I don't have anymore. But she's got plenty of life left in her yet. Couldn't see letting her rot away in a damn marina. That's why I sold her. It's your turn to live a dream."

The young man smiled. "You can bet I'll take care of her. She'll be carrying me around the world."

Thelma's head drooped with every word she heard. Tears welled in her eyes and she stared down at her fluffy pink slippers.

Theodora cocked her hip, arched her brows and gave Thelma a wry smile.

The colonel scratched the side of his neck and squinted up at the young man. "I couldn't help noticing you changed her name. It can be bad luck you know, especially in a vessel this age. You might want to reconsider."

Thelma held her breath. *Listen to the man!*

The new owner shoved his hands in the pockets of his jeans. "I gave it a lot of thought, but decided she deserved a classier name. And frankly, I'd be uncomfortable crossing the Pacific in a boat named *'THELMA'*. The name just doesn't inspire confidence."

The colonel clucked his tongue and sighed, "Class has nothin' to do with it, son. You need something you can depend on. Believe me, after forty years sailing her, I should know." He held out his hand. "But you're the captain." He shook hands with the new owner. "Good luck, Matt. You've got my e-mail—keep me in your travel loop. I wish you fair winds and following seas." Then he stepped onto the dock.

Chapter 2

All her years at sea hadn't prepared Thelma for anything like this. None of her finely honed sailing skills could help her now. This wasn't a thundering North Atlantic storm or a deadly lee shore, but it was shallow water indeed.

She'd been built in a reputable English yard steeped in nautical tradition. The thought of someone actually changing her name had never crossed her mind. Of course she hadn't counted on being sailed to America. Everyone knew the Yanks changed all the rules, but she had felt safe with the colonel. She even enjoyed the warm waters in Ft. Lauderdale. How could he abandon her like this? After all she'd done for him. And now to be kicked out by this...this floozy. *queen my arse! If she's a queen, then I'm the Britannia.*

"Well, Thelma, time to pack your bags."

Theodora's words cut through her reverie like an icy Baltic Sea wave. The witch had already started to unpack.

Thelma glanced at her transom. The geezer had just put the final stroke on the royal 'R' and was sitting back admiring his handiwork. It now read: THEODORA R. Thelma wanted to scream.

But just one minute. Why am I still here? A bit pale maybe, but definitely still here. She noticed Theodora staring at her.

The queen had paused in her unpacking. "Why don't you make yourself scarce? It's my name on the transom now. You know the drill. I'm in, you're out. Time to fade babe."

Thelma looked down at the front of her robe and held her arms out. The transformation had ceased. She had stopped fading. She lifted her gaze to the queen. If she wasn't mistaken, Theodora still hadn't filled out as one might expect. Her figure had the same substance as her own, of someone not quite whole.

The Queen's eyes narrowed. "What are you up to, you old bat? She jerked a thumb toward her chest. "I'm the boat now. I want you out!"

The shock of waking up to the betrayal of the colonel and the imminent loss of her identity had momentarily backed Thelma's sails but now she was gathering wind. It finally dawned on her why she and the queen were stuck in irons. She began to giggle and covered her mouth, but the mirth boiled over until she clasped her belly and roared with laughter.

Theodora watched with a sneer. She crossed her arms on her chest. "Care to let me in on the joke?"

Thelma caught her breath, wiped tears from her eyes. "Oh, lordy lordy," she huffed and cocked a finger at the queen. "Come with me, Missy, there's something you have to see." She led Theodora through the engine room, into the main cabin and past the galley to the forepeak, stroking her oiled teak interior as she went. She perched one haunch on the double bunk beneath the forward hatch and patted the mattress. "Have a sit, Missy."

Theodora glanced suspiciously at Thelma, then reluctantly sat beside her, tucking her long white gown between her knees.

Thelma pointed to a stout oak deck beam just forward of the mast. It was a good five inches square, varnished to a brilliant luster and arched across eight feet from thwart to thwart. Carved deeply into the beam by a skilled hand was, THELMA # 102406. "That's me, Missy, and my British registration. It'll take more than a coat of paint and some fancy letters to make me disappear. Where I come from they build 'em to last."

Theodora frowned and tapped her thumbnail against her front teeth. "You mean, as long as your name is carved in that beam you'll be around?"

Thelma slapped a meaty thigh. "As sure as there's caulk in my seams, Missy."

Theodora's pale complexion sunk below a wave of red. She spoke through clenched teeth. "Count your days, honey. No way I'm sharing this hull with you." She jumped up and stormed aft.

Thelma smiled after her co-spirit, delighted she'd put the pretentious wench in her place. As far as she was concerned, a shared hull was far better than none at all. She reached up with a calloused hand and felt the life in her name.

Above deck, Matt Priest peeled back an inch of varnished cotton twine that covered the wire splice on the port shroud. He didn't like what he saw. The strands of galvanized rigging were thick with rust, and if there was one thing he hated, it was rust. He spoke to the boat as if she were human. "This'll have to go, sweetheart. I've got a deal lined up for a whole new set of stainless rigging for you. Can't trust this old junk to hold up your mast. When I'm through, you'll be a class act."

He pulled a small notebook from his back pocket and started his list of priorities. Rigging was at the top, followed by an upgrade of the electrical wiring. As nice as the old colonel was, he hadn't known squat about electricity. The wiring in the engine room was a nightmare. Engine parts, steering cables and re-galvanizing the anchor chain ran down the page. And right at the bottom, veneer for carved deck beam.

He planned to be at sea within the month. Barring any unpleasant surprises when he hauled Theodora to paint her bottom, it would happen. He wanted to sail out of Port Everglades on his thirtieth birthday. He hoped it would be a big event, with friends and family escorting him past the breakwater.

Matt scratched thoughtfully at the new stubble on his chin—the start of his sailor's beard—and thought about his girlfriend, Sara. She should be here soon, if she didn't have to work late. Her family ran an antique shop downtown and it took most of her time. She still hadn't made up her mind about whether she would join him on the adventure. Matt couldn't understand why she didn't jump at the chance. But he knew better than to push too hard. Sara had to be eased into anything new.

Thelma watched him with a measuring eye as he sat in the contoured helmsman's seat and gripped the wheel. He gave it a turn then caressed the oiled teak spokes. Matt's obvious affection for the boat almost outweighed his ignorance in changing the name, but Thelma wasn't quite ready to forgive him that blunder. She studied his movements, realizing that although he was no old salt, the potential for a fine sailor was there.

She sensed the boy would take some watching and was worried about the influence of Theodora. She'd seen the little queen preening at the prospect of new stainless steel rigging and felt Matt's repugnance for rust. Not that rust was a good thing, mind you, but it had its place. For Thelma, that place was in the rigging. Stainless steel might look bright and shiny, but there was a price to pay. The vain qualities that kept it rust free were the same that hid its weak spots and caused it to let go without warning. Her old galvanized rigging, weeping tears of oxidized iron as it aged, was as honest and forthright as the craftsmen who laid her keel. There was never any doubt when the stuff was tired, giving a sailor plenty of time to replace it.

Matt reached over and gave the bronze ship's bell a ring. He scowled at its dull, greenish hue, then rooted around in a cockpit locker until he came up with an old can of polishing compound. The colonel hadn't been much of a spit and polish man and there was little aboard that carried a high shine. Matt lifted the bell from its mounting, padded on a dab of the pungent red paste and commenced to rub.

Thelma smiled indulgently at the boy's misdirected priorities, but at the same time she was pleased, because the ship's bell had been a christening gift from her builders. She felt a slight nudge from behind and turned to find the queen.

"Just another indication that your time is up, Thelma. I'll be in the spotlight as soon as Matt makes a few changes."

Thelma ignored her, refusing to give Theodora the satisfaction of a response. *Another minute now and you'll eat those words, Missy.* She noticed a thin sheen of perspiration on Matt's forehead and heard his breath turn to a pant as he ground the dull green to a lustrous gold. His biceps bulged, stretching his T-shirt. It wasn't until he rotated the bell and the engraved letters of her name stood out like scrimshaw, that Thelma spoke to her hull-mate. "Now don't that just fiddle your rails, eh, luv?"

Theodora let out a long hiss that sounded like she'd sprung a leak, gave Thelma a look that could melt the tar in a deck seam and receded to her royal quarters in the stern.

Thelma felt pity more than intolerance for Theodora. What a shame to be burdened with an ego like that. At the rate she was going, she'd look an old woman before the planned voyage was over.

Matt disappointed Thelma once again by remounting the now brilliant bell with her name facing the bulkhead instead of the cockpit. She gave a deep sigh, resigned to the notion that she'd need a world of patience with the boy. She heard a faint laugh from the queen. Thelma rolled her eyes. *And with her, too.*

Chapter 3

Matt was below, taking measurements off the deck beam that had Thelma's name carved into it when he heard the sharp clack of Sara's shoes on deck. "Shoes!" he bellowed.

Silence, then the soft pad of bare feet. Sara's blonde head appeared in the companionway, smiling blue eyes. "Sorry about that. I forgot."

"Plays hell with wood decks," Matt said. "And it's very poor boat etiquette."

She gave him a mock salute and lowered her voice. "I promise to do better, Captain."

Matt laughed. "See that you do or it's thirty lashes with the cat."

She climbed down the companionway ladder, her soft, undefined legs moving with caution. Dressed in immaculate white pleated shorts and V-neck T-shirt, blatantly defying the gods of grime, she sat primly on the port settee, a roll of papers in her hand. "Whatcha doin'?"

"I want to make an oak veneer to cover this old name and registration number."

Until then, Thelma had been mildly curious about what Matt was up to and had even been applauding his concern for her decks. Now she stood in shocked dismay, wanting to reach out and deliver a hearty slap alongside his head. *What could the boy be thinking?*

Theodora came to gloat. In a poor attempt at mimicking Thelma's voice she said, "Don't that just fiddle your rails, hey, luv?"

In a rare moment of anger born of frustration and despair, Thelma lashed out. "Hush, you hussy!"

In a parody of a mortal wound, Theodora clutched her heart and swooned. "Such language! You slay me, granny. And like I said, when Matt's finished, so are you."

Sara stepped into the forepeak to see what Matt was talking about. When she saw the finely carved letters and numbers, she looked puzzled. "Why do you want to cover those up?"

"Her name's *Theodora R* now, registered in Florida with a new number. I'm giving her a complete face lift."

"But the original name and number are important historical references. They're the boat's heritage," Sara pointed out. "It would be like removing a significant provenance on an antique. You'd be lowering her value."

Thelma wanted to give the girl a big hug. *Oh, you beauty.* Matt stopped his note taking and thought about what Sara had said. "I like that," he said. "I was thinking it was like a constant reminder of what this boat used to be, which hadn't included me. But what you say makes sense...and it'll save me a bunch of work."

Thelma looked at Theodora, who appeared ready to rip out Sara's hair. "You were saying, luv?"

Theodora glowered, holding her fingers like osprey talons. "I had a feeling the bitch would be trouble," she grumbled, then thrust her face an inch from Thelma's nose. "If we're stuck here together, just keep your distance."

Sara held up the papers she'd brought below. "Remember when I asked you about the name Theodora?"

"Sure," Matt said. "What about it?"

"Well, you were right, she was co-ruler of Rome with King Justinian around four-hundred A.D., and definitely a very powerful woman. But there's more to the story. I did a little research on the queen and came up with a lot of juicy stuff."

She had Matt's attention...and Thelma's. Theodora sat at the table in the main cabin, legs crossed, filing her nails.

Sara giggled. "Did you know she was known as the whore of Babylon?"

Matt made a wry face. "The whore of Babylon?" Jesus, he could imagine how she got that name.

She tapped the papers. "According to this biography I got from a book about famous women, she was the daughter of some peasant that trained bears or something and literally screwed her way to the throne."

Matt patted the forward bulkhead. "She's one classy broad, ain't she?"

Thelma glanced at Theodora, not bothering to hide the disapproval.

Theodora looked up from her nails. "They won't find *you* in a book of famous women."

"It gets better. Listen to this," Sara said. "The young queen had a unique way of dealing with her opposition. Under the guise of friendship, she would invite those known to have spoken against her to a gala feast where the wine flowed freely. After the festivities, when all were sleepy and wits dulled, Theodora's loyal guards would enter the pavilion and slaughter the scores of guests." Sara glanced up from her reading. "She was a class act, all right."

Thelma was aghast, horrified that she'd be sharing her hull with...with a monster. "You did that?" she whispered, not wanting to hear the answer.

Theodora spread a thick coat of blood-red lacquer on her thumbnail. She blew on it with pursed lips. "They exaggerate. I only did that once and there were only a dozen or so. The sea of politics was a treacherous place in those days. It was my way of reaching a safe harbor."

The casual, seemingly unconcerned air in which the queen dismissed the murder of a dozen people was beyond Thelma's comprehension. The attitude, more than the deed, made her shiver. All she could do was stare open-mouthed and shake her head.

"Look at it this way," Matt said. "She's a survivor."

"And that's supposed to instill confidence?"

"Well, hey, how would you feel if you'd discovered Theodora was a wimp? That would have made Thelma look good."

Sara mulled that over. "Yeah, you've got a point."

For Thelma, it was all too clear what a survivor the little queen was. Sharks would fare poorly if the dear were cast adrift. The only thing Thelma had left to guarantee her existence was the deck beam where her name was carved. There was no doubt Theodora would do her damnedest to see it gone. She knew it would take watch-on-watch and a weather eye for foul play if the queen wasn't to scuttle her berth.

Chapter 4

Matt took Theodora's biography from Sara and scanned it briefly. He huffed a laugh and sat beside her on the bunk. "Should make for some good bedtime reading." He rubbed the back of Sara's neck then pulled her closer. "I'm glad you looked this stuff up. It tells me you're interested."

She nibbled his earlobe. "It's you I'm interested in, not the boat."

Thelma frowned.

Theodora gave a derisive snort. "I could have told you that."

Matt held Sara by the shoulders and looked her in the eye. "Better get used to it, she's my home now."

It took a moment to sink in, then came Sara's sharp gasp. "You sold your house?"

Matt grinned and his eyebrows almost arched to his hairline. "Closed today. It's a done deal."

Sara collapsed back on the bunk, hands over her face. "My God, you're really going to do this."

Her reaction spun Matt into confusion. "Hey, I've been talking about a circumnavigation for a couple of years now. I told you when I found the right boat it would happen."

Sara took her hands from her face. Tears left shiny tracks to her ears. She stared at the deck-planking overhead. "I...I was hoping it was a passing fancy...something you'd get over."

"Passing fancy?" He fought to keep his voice down. "When have I ever had a passing fancy? You've known me long enough to know I'm not a bullshitter. Of course I'm going sailing." He reached over, wiped a tear from her face with his thumb and whispered, "Come with me." He wanted desperately for her to join him, share in the adventure. Her reluctance drove him nuts.

She blinked once. "You make it sound so easy. Just drop everything and go sailing. It's...it's not that simple for me."

"Listen to her snivel," Theodora said. "You'd think he'd asked her to perform some degrading sex act."

Thelma, amazed that she could still be shocked by anything the queen said, clucked her tongue. "Good lord, Missy, you've got a heart as hard as oak knots. A life at sea is difficult to fathom for those not born to it."

"Ease your sheets, granny. She's the last thing we need."

Thelma pulled in the slack on the frayed line she used to hold her robe closed and deftly tied a square knot with a loop. "I agree she might not be the ideal first mate, but the sweet thing is important to Matt. And a happy captain makes a happy ship."

Theodora made a sour face. "I swear I'll puke if I hear another sappy platitude."

Matt took Sara's hands and pulled her to her feet. "What's the problem? Don't you want to go?"

Sara thought for a second. "If that's what it takes to be with you, yes. But I have other issues, like money, my folks, the lease on my apartment..."

Matt didn't like what he was hearing. These were old arguments they'd flogged around the fleet. There was plenty of money for both him and Sara and he'd made it clear that whatever she could contribute would be gravy. Anyway, money had never been a problem. The sale of his house helped, but the long-term money would come from his partner who had offered to buy Matt's half of the flourishing landscape business they'd started in high school.

From what he knew of her folks, they'd be supportive of anything Sara wanted to do and they had run the antique shop for years without her.

According to the real estate agent that sold Matt's house, there was a housing shortage that would take care of Sara's apartment lease.

Sara's was the voice of someone without desire. Matt knew it, but was loathe to accept it. He wanted to grab her shoulders, shake her and yell, "Doesn't the adventure excite you? Sailing to foreign lands? The challenge of the sea?" Instead he let it ride, afraid to push, afraid she'd shut the door. He'd never really thought in terms of a solo adventure. The scenario was always a shared experience. Maybe it was time to explore the possibility of a singlehanded cruise.

He opened the bottle of Australian cabernet he'd bought to celebrate the first meal aboard. He handed Sara a glass, then proposed a toast. "Here's to thirty days and counting to castoff."

She gave him a weak smile that said, *I'm afraid to commit and you know it.*

The meal, spaghetti with a canned sauce, lacked the excitement and spirit of a looming grand adventure that would have made it a success. Sara made excuses to leave early.

Matt shrugged it off. He knew better than to press, deciding to let the impending deadline tighten the screws.

Thelma waited for Sara to climb out the companionway hatch then used what little worldly power she had to swing the clapper on her newly polished bell.

The unexpected ring made Sara jump and she glanced around. Her eye caught the exposed portion of Thelma's engraved name. "Matt, can I turn the bell around so we see the old name?"

"Sure," he said. "If we're keeping the name up forward, you might as well."

Sara gripped the flare of the bell and rotated it so THELMA showed brightly to the world.

"You're encouraging her," snapped Theodora. "She'll be an albatross around Matt's neck and I'll bet you the lead in my keel she won't keep up my brightwork." The queen made use of her own powers. Surreptitiously, she eased the topping lift where it was cleated off on the pin-rail and her weighty fir boom dropped a few treacherous inches.

Sara stepped from the cockpit and cracked her forehead on the boom. She collapsed onto a cockpit bench, slapped a hand to her skull and groaned.

Matt leapt up the companionway ladder. "Jesus, Babe, you okay?" *Damn, I thought I had the boom well clear.* He sat beside her and tried to pull her hand away. "Let's get some ice on it."

Sara turned away, cursing the boat from between clenched teeth. "It's okay," she said, but tears welled up like a spring tide.

Matt, at a loss for anything else to do, wrapped her in his arms, and rocked her gently.

Thelma peered at the queen with narrowed eyes. She had a sneaking suspicion the wench had been up to a bit of deviltry, but she'd known the topping lift to slip in the past.

Theodora observed Sara's misery with a bemused sneer then glanced at Thelma. "Pity."

The next few weeks ran together like a well-spliced line. Theodora and Thelma felt a settling in their waterline as Matt shipped aboard a steady stream of tools, boat gear and ship's stores. Gasket sets, spare engine parts, spools of line, canned goods and a sewing machine crammed the abundant locker space.

Both spirits delighted in the lavish cosmetics stored in the paint locker: oil-based enamels, honey-thick varnish and rich teak oil. They ogled over the precious boxes of bronze and stainless steel fastenings.

Matt kept his appointment with the shipyard and had *THEODORA R* hauled out for new bottom paint and general maintenance below the waterline. Her robust hull and traditional construction that showed off the full-length pitchpine planks excited a constant flow of compliments from other yachties at the yard.

One old-timer named Zeke had the only other wooden boat in the yard. He was a willing source of wooden boat remedies and arcane nautical wisdom. Matt looked forward to his early morning visits and always had a fresh cup of coffee ready.

Theodora basked in the limelight and it seemed to Thelma that the queen's hips took on a sway that could roll her mast out.

Thelma kept a sharp eye on the work Matt performed on her hull. If he didn't hammer home a cotton seam 'til it rings', she would spit it out during the night. Next morning, Matt would find strands of twisted cotton dangling from her hull.

Sara made daily appearances, but she never once picked up a paintbrush or a piece of sandpaper. Her sole contribution was to praise Matt's work and make a dinner or lunch for him. Although willing to eat, he was too fixated on weepy seams, greasing through-hull fittings and laying on new paint to bother with preparing food.

Thelma felt sorry for Matt, who still spoke in terms of *we* when talking to Sara about the cruise. Sara remained steadfastly noncommittal and only once spent the night aboard. Her behavior brought tedious waves of smug remarks from the queen. Thelma wanted to caulk her mouth shut. Yesterday's brief visit from Sara had brought an especially crass response from Theodora. "What's he see in the trollop, anyway? She's got great T&A, but a lotta good it does him. She's only stayed one night since he moved aboard."

"Stow it!" Thelma had said. "The girl needs time." Unfortunately, time was running out and Thelma had a sinking feeling that Sara would literally miss the boat.

The day finally came for the two coats of new anti-fouling paint, heavy copper-based red stuff that smelled like burnt cork and always made Thelma croon and drool with desire.

Theodora, although pleased, said she preferred the blue.

Sara showed up in ratty, gray Oshkosh coveralls.

"Bless her soul," Thelma declared.

Theodora snorted. "Hold the blessing 'til she picks up a roller."

Matt was surprised, too. "Hey, you look like someone looking for work."

Sara leaned over and picked up a roller. "I am. I just gave notice at my other job."

Matt stared, afraid to break the silence. "You mean...

She nodded.

Matt let out a whoop, scooped her in his arms and swung her about. Their laughter carried over the sound of power tools in the yard and Thelma thankfully missed what she presumed was another vile remark from the queen.

Two days after *THEODORA R* was lowered back in the water and four days before his thirtieth birthday, the expected day of departure, Matt arrived with coils of stainless rigging wire and boxes of turnbuckles and terminal ends. He handed the lot to Sara, who stood ready in the cockpit, then said, "That's everything she'll need, but I don't think we'll be ready in four days."

Thelma, poised to replace a bobby pin in one of her curlers, paused and cocked her head. Something Matt had said didn't ring quite true.

Even Sara seemed to pick up on it. "Why not? We've got all the measurements and you said it would only take a couple of days."

Matt surveyed the pile of rigging and his gaze drifted up the mast. "Well, that might have been wishful thinking."

"But what about your birthday? Everyone's expecting us to leave. We'll have an escort worthy of the queen."

"We might have to cancel," he said abruptly.

She shrugged one shoulder. "You're the captain."

It was the first time Thelma had heard Matt say anything resembling a negative. Any problems had merely been a challenge that Matt seemed to lust after. Why such a big to-do about the rigging?

Theodora was too infatuated with her shiny new rigging to care.

Chapter 5

As the new rigging was cut to length and fit in place, Thelma grudgingly admitted that it did add a certain elegance to her appearance. The queen, however, fairly swooned over each new length of glistening cable and tittered over the finely machined terminal ends that Matt attached.

"This is no silver tiara," Thelma told the queen. "You'd best keep an eye on our Matt and see that each piece is a proper fit and that he pins all our bottlescrews. We can't have them backing off and losing tension. It just won't do."

Theodora paused in her constant primping and gave an exasperated sigh. She set down the mirror that seemed to be a permanent fixture in her right hand. "Cut him some slack you old fuddy-duddy. He's got a grip on things."

Thelma held her tongue. She did tend to meddle, but it was usually for the captain's own good. She was concerned about Matt's lack of wind in getting her ready for sea. And he was certainly taking his time with this rigging job—more than it deserved. It seemed the boy kept forgetting odds and ends, running off in that truck of his and wasting precious hours for some frivolous gadget. This morning it was a packet of bright, red plastic strips he thought he needed for telltales. Why, any sailor worth his salt would use thin strips of wool. The red plastic might tell one where the wind was coming from, but it was too artificial for her tastes, not in keeping with her class of yacht. Of course the queen was ecstatic over the silly baubles. They matched her nail polish.

Sara could easily run these silly errands for the boy. In fact, she'd heard the dear girl offer to fetch the items, but Matt insisted on doing it himself. She couldn't help thinking he was delaying things on purpose.

That evening, two days before his birthday, Matt fired up the gas grill mounted on Theodora's sternrail. "Steaks tonight," he announced. "Grab a bottle of wine from the bilge, Sara. We deserve a break."

Sara glanced at the sun, then at the new forestay lying on the jetty. It was ready for mounting. "Why stop now? We have plenty of daylight left. We can call out for a pizza later." She picked up one end of the cable. "We'll have this up before dark. Let's not waste the time."

"It's not a waste of time. Think of it as a shift toward cruising mode, a slower pace of life, quality not quantity."

She placed her fists on her hips and gave Matt a puzzled look. "What's come over you? A week ago you were cracking the whip like Captain Bligh and now we're in Margaritaville. I busted my buns to get all my stuff aboard and tie up loose ends for the big send-off. Now you act like we could damn well take our time and to hell with departure dates. What's it going to be?"

He hadn't expected a confrontation and was at a loss to explain himself. He shut the gas valve with a vicious twist, hopped to the jetty and faced Sara. "I was just trying to...to...oh, hell, you wouldn't understand." He whirled and marched off.

Thelma watched Sara stare after him as he disappeared in the direction of the shipyard. "I believe our Matt is sailing uncharted waters."

Theodora pointed toward Sara. "It's her fault. The sun's below the yardarm. She needs to relax, learn to party. Matt was only trying to help."

Thelma turned on the queen. "What would you know about it, Missy? You're so full of yourself and that bloody mirror we could drag anchor and be on the beach before you'd notice."

Matt didn't know where he was going, except to get away. He followed the path his feet took while his brain waited for a lull in the mental squall. For several days now he'd felt like a light-wind sail in a rising breeze and the pressure was getting to him. So far, he'd been unable to pinpoint its source. At first he attributed it to the weight of command and the responsibility that comes with taking a vessel to sea. But hell, he was used to being the boss. His landscape business had forty-seven employees and that was a hell of a responsibility. He knew he'd been creating excuses not to get the work done. His partner would call it Avoidance Behavior. Matt called it Dragging Ass.

The shriek of a router biting into hardwood shocked Matt out of his daze. He shook his head to clear his mind, then realized he'd wandered into the back row at the shipyard, close to where *THEODORA R* had been. The metallic smells of bottom paint and wood preservative tickled his nose. He saw old Zeke working in the shade of his forty-foot trawler. Matt smiled to himself, thinking if the scrawny weathered fisherman was lying on the beach, he could pass for driftwood.

He crunched across the gravel and watched Zeke spread maroon-colored glue on thin planks of mahogany. Two lame sawhorses did a shaky job of holding up the strips. Matt reached out and steadied the nearest one. Zeke glanced up, but didn't say anything, just continued to squeegee the puddles of glue with a scrap of cardboard. Matt stood mesmerized by the hypnotic back and forth action of the old mariner's hand.

"Are you a spreader or a glob-n-press man?" Zeke finally asked. His voice sounded like a rusty nail being pulled from wet wood.

It took a second for Matt to realize he'd been spoken to and another to understand the question. "Spreader," he said.

Zeke fitted the two strips together and twisted on a couple of 'C' clamps. Glue oozed from the seams. "I used to be glob-n-press, but I had some failures where the glue hadn't got to. Hasn't happened since I started spreadin'.."

Without thinking, Matt asked. "You ever uncomfortable about going to sea?" As soon as it was out, he felt embarrassed and he knew his face had flushed red.

Zeke went about the clamping process, wiping off dribbles of glue with his fingers. "Uncomfortable?" he mused. "I think the word you're lookin' for is right up there with scared shitless." He never looked at Matt, but kept talking. "I seen you wasn't gettin' nowhere with your riggin'. Wondered 'bout that."

Matt sighed and shoved his hands into his back pockets. "That obvious is it?"

Zeke wiped his hands on the sides of his pants then looked Matt in the eye. "Ain't a bad thing to be scared. Gives ya' a healthy respect for the sea." He stepped over to a paint-spattered white cooler, flipped up the lid and pulled out a couple cans of Miller Lite. He tossed one to Matt. "Half the guys in this yard are just fiddlin' with their boats so's they don't have to go back out. Marinas are full of guys installin' worthless gadgets to put off leavin' harbor."

Matt popped the lid on his beer and took a swig. *God, does he ever have me pegged.* "So, how do you get over it?"

Zeke tipped his can up, let the beer gurgle down his gullet, then set the empty can on the cooler. He burped. "If you're lucky, you never will. The trick is, as I see it anyways, is to focus on the first half mile."

Matt puzzled over that. "First half mile?"

"Yep, that'll usually get you past the breakwater."

Matt thought about that for a minute then grinned. "Sure, then you're out!"

"Ten feet, ten miles, across the Atlantic, out is out." Zeke winked and laughed like a Disney pirate.

Matt roared right along with him until his side ached and tears ran down his face. The pressure wasn't gone, but at least he knew what it was. Intimidation had slowly set in at the thought of ten years at sea on a round-the-world, fifty-thousand mile cruise. But now, thanks to the old mariner, it was only a matter of the first half-mile. He finished off the beer, gave Zeke a thumbs-up and sprinted toward the marina.

Sara was still on the jetty, kneeling, measuring another length of cable. He slowed to a walk and approached her with a fragile grin. She pretended to be busy. "Sorry," Matt said. "I had a little self-confidence problem, but I think I'm over it." *I'll know in a couple of days.*

She didn't look up. "So what's it going to be, wine and grilled steaks or pizza?"

Matt smiled. "If you hurry with that cable, we can have the fore and back stays up before dark... and pizza's fine."

She leapt up and gave him a hug. "Nice to have you back, Captain Bligh."

Thelma had just taken a bite of a scone and spoke with her mouth full. "Did you hear that?" It came out 'Dood you her tha?' She swallowed. "Sounds like the boy found himself a pilot."

21

Theodora flicked a crumb off her white robe. "I'd rather he was still lost. I was looking forward to the sundowner crowd and entertainment on the foredeck."

Ain't that just like the little queen. If it was up to her, all we'd be is a showboat.

Chapter 6

Matt's birthday cleared the horizon on February eighteenth, with the promise of a fair weather departure. Aboard the *THEODORA R*, chaos reigned. The previous night's final provisioning made below decks look like a Caribbean wharf on mail-boat day. It smelled like a supermarket.

They tested the limits of physical laws, coaxing thirty pounds of produce into a twenty-pound space. Hanging from the deck beams, a bulging hammock of bananas, cabbage, tomatoes, eggplant and cucumbers swung ominously over the dining table. They stuffed sacks of potatoes and onions into odd-shaped lockers under their bunk up-forward. Flour, sugar, pasta, beans and rice were still homeless along with a precarious skyline of boxed goods, beer and eggs.

"Roaches!" Thelma raved. "Didn't anyone tell the captain about bringing cardboard boxes aboard. Mark my words, Missy. We'll have roaches by the score if he don't get those boxes ashore. Full of the buggers, they are."

Theodora, who was applying a touch of green eyeliner, tilted her mirror so she could see Thelma's face. "Did you say roaches...as in cockroaches?"

The indigo in Theodora's eyes was purged by the flair of her pupils, and it was the first time Thelma had heard trepidation in the queen's voice. *Payback time.* "Oh Lord, Missy, if he don't get rid of those boxes, we'll be infested with the bloody creatures. They'll take over the night and there's nothing they like better than an old wood boat. We won't get a moment's peace with all their scurrying about."

Theodora made a vile face. "Sharing this space with you is bad enough. No way I'll put up with those creepy bugs. Just thinking about all those hairy legs tickling my bilge makes me wanna scream."

Temptation won out and Thelma carried on. "Down-island they call 'em mahogany birds and that's just where we're headed. Big

23

they are—almost afraid to step on 'em for fear they'll take my foot off."

The queen paled and Thelma chuckled to herself. *A few roaches might be worth it to see the hussy squirm.*

Matt looked around the cabin, silently calculating. It felt like there was a bucket of live shrimp in his belly. Castoff time would be two o'clock if all went as planned, but the to-do list seemed endless. He checked off 'fresh food' even though they hadn't even yet coated the eggs with Vaseline. "We've made a dent, but there's still a lot left on the list. Let's do the eggs and then we'll take her over to the fuel jetty."

Sara stuck her head out of the small aft cabin, her face flush from wrestling with fifty pounds of flour. "You really think it's worth the trouble?"

He nodded. "That's what the books say. Keep out the air and they'll last six months."

"Why didn't he read the part about cockroaches?" Theodora asked to no one in particular.

"Where do you want the beer?" Sara asked.

"The bilge. Without a fridge, bilge-cool is the best we can do."

She looked skeptical. "The lack of cold beer is going to be a challenge for me. And what about you and your frosted mugs?"

"We'll get over it." Matt said. "Half the people in the yard were repairing or replacing fridges. That's one headache I don't need."

She shot him a look. "Oookaaay, but that hot day in the tropics will come when you'll kill for ice."

"Hmph! Fat chance." Matt gathered up the empty boxes, tossed them through the hatch and into the cockpit then followed them out and hauled the lot to the dumpster. He knew he shouldn't have brought them aboard, but the threat of cockroaches seemed blown out of proportion and the boxes made the provisioning a whole lot easier.

"Took him long enough." Theodora said. "If we have any crawly brown stowaways aboard I'll mutiny."

Thelma's back stiffened, her hands trembled and a roller popped loose from her hair and clattered into the bilge. She stepped up to the queen and poked a finger in her chest. "Don't you *ever* use that 'M' word around me again." Her voice fairly shook. "I can tolerate scuttlebutt like any jack before the mast, but I'll not stand for that."

Shocked by Thelma's rage, Theodora held up both hands. "It was a joke, okay? A joke."

"We never joke about that, Missy, you hear?"

"Well excuuuuse me for springing your planks, Thelma, but how should I know you can't handle the 'M' word."

Thelma clutched at the collar of her robe. The anger simmered like a confused sea after a storm. She turned her back to the queen and shuffled forward to the privacy of the chain locker. There had been a time when the idea of mutiny was a distant sea tale and hadn't aroused passion in Thelma, but that was some forty years ago. The golden time before she lost her first owner, the loving man who had commissioned her. She mourned his passing as though it were yesterday.

The memory of the pre-dawn disaster was as vivid as blue ice. A summer's cruise round southern Ireland in '74 had gone sour when her owner, the captain, discovered a cache of firearms aboard. Thelma had done her best, letting the mainsheet fly so her boom swept the mutinous cook over the side. But the damage had been done. Her owner, bleeding from a knife wound, fought heavy seas in a raging gale to save her from the hungry rocks off the Irish shore. She could still see those black teeth and hear the sea's foaming madness, lusting for her hull. Her captain's valiant efforts had ultimately cost the dear man his life, all for another man's dubious cause.

The rumble of the diesel brought Thelma out of her funk.

Matt, using hand signals he and Sara had worked out, motioned for her to cast off the bow-line. He let loose the stern, engaged the prop and they thrumped fifty yards across the channel to the fuel jetty.

Theodora was in a panic over Sara's placement of her fenders. "Can't she see they're too low? I'll lose paint off my tumblehome if Matt brings us in too fast."

Thelma had never heard anyone fret over cosmetics like the queen. Ever since Matt had taken the oxalic acid to her topside paint and brought back the shine, she'd been a royal pain in the bum. If it wasn't the fenders, it was the wake of a passing boat or a dinghy coming along side. *Heavens, you'd think a scratch would sink her.* Thelma had grown comfortable with what the colonel had called the thirty-foot look, and from thirty feet she knew she looked a stunner. She wondered how long Matt would satisfy the queen's desire for the two-foot look.

But Matt had spent too much time getting *THEODORA R* shipshape in Bristol fashion to risk a scratch. He laid her alongside with a lovers touch.

Theodora threw him a kiss. "My man."

Thelma was proud of the boy. In some ways, Matt reminded her of her first owner. His attention to detail and the way he doted on her needs were surely reminiscent. Whether it was laying on a coat of varnish for her spruce mast or splicing a length of fir into a soft spot on her deck, Matt's caress was as gentle as a zephyr in the doldrums.

By the time Matt and Sara had topped up the fuel and water tanks it was pushing noon, and well-wishers had begun to arrive at the marina. The festive nature of the occasion seemed to bring out the flamboyant side of everyone's personality. The young Cuban man running the fuel pump was so distracted by two babes in string bikinis, red spiked heels, and tiny sailor hats that he dribbled a slick of diesel oil down the deck.

Thelma wrinkled her nose at the pungent odor and covered her ears to block out the queen's whining. "That's enough, Missy, we're prettier than the day I was launched and a dollop of oil won't spoil our deck."

Sara, having gone ashore to dump more garbage, hopped aboard. Her boat shoes hit the slick.

Both spirits cringed when she crashed to the deck.

She rolled to her side, breath clearly knocked out of her.

Matt, who had just ducked below for a bottle of Joy dishwashing soap to clean the spill, burst from the companionway. "What th...? Sara?" He rushed to her side.

"Won't spoil the day, huh?" Theodora said. "Sure knocked the wind out of her sails."

"Humph!" Thelma said. "I can tell you're terribly broken up about it. Would it kill you to show a wee bit of sympathy?"

"I'll say it again," the queen said. "She doesn't have our best interests at heart."

"Your interests, you mean." Thelma stalked off and perched on the end of her bowsprit.

Matt helped Sara to her feet. "Easy on the deck there, girl." His attempt at humor earned him a wry look.

She rubbed her hip and elbow. "I hope my folks didn't see that. They've already commented on my bruise collection. My dad thinks I belong in a home for battered women."

He doused the deck with Joy then scrubbed off the diesel.

Theodora acted as if she were fresh from a shower. "Oooh, that felt good."

"We smell like lemons now," Thelma said.

Back at their slip, a party of thirty or so people had gathered, all dressed as if for a costume ball with a nautical theme. Matt conned the boat into the berth, shut the engine down and tossed the stern line to Captain Hook.

Matt's business partner, dressed as Popeye, stepped aboard with an open bottle of champagne. "It ain't spinach, but it won't turn the decks green if we spill it."

Matt waved an arm toward the crowd. "I see your hand in this."

"Ay Cap'n, but 'twas you wanted a party."

Theodora clapped and bounced on her toes. "This is more like it! Party-time, old girl. Break out your dancing shoes."

Thelma, whose idea of a wild party was a lively game of whist, ignored the queen. But in honor of the occasion she whipped the ends of the rope at her waist into tight figure eights.

Matt's father, who wore a plumed commodore's hat and long-tailed coat, hailed from the jetty. "Permission to come aboard, Captain."

Matt chuckled to himself. It was the first time he'd ever heard his father ask permission for anything. He helped his old man to the deck. "Permission granted."

His father held out a slip of paper. "Winds SSE 12-15 knots," was scribbled in a shaky hand.

"Met report," his father said. "Good for twelve hours. A cold front is supposed to blow through tomorrow—northwest winds to thirty knots."

Matt stuffed the paper in his pocket. "Good window. We should be in the northern Bahamas by then."

An awkward silence followed, then his father threw an arm around Matt's shoulders. "I'm proud of you, Son. Takes real guts to follow your dream."

The display choked Matt up for a moment. "Thanks, Dad. I'll keep in touch with e-mails and the odd postcard. I have a laptop and digital camera so I can send pics as well."

Thelma wiped a tear from the corner of her eye. "Don't that just wring your sails."

"Oh, spare me," the queen said. "Matt's embarrassed as hell and his old man looks like a clown. If you want something to cry about, take a look forward. Sara's mother just stepped aboard with high heels."

The tide of friends and family soon had the decks awash. Old Zeke showed up for a farewell beer dressed in his usual ancient fisherman's garb right down to the sea boots and tattered sou'wester. Matt's buddies awarded him a bottle of wine for best costume.

Sara's folks brought several trays of sandwiches. Matt figured he'd be cleaning yellow globs of egg salad off the decks for a week. But hell, today he didn't care. He felt on top of the world. The work had gotten done on time, his lady was aboard and in a short time they'd sail out of here with the grace of a dolphin.

Thelma endured their lack of manners with a tolerant smile, despite the gravel, oil and dirt tracked aboard. Thankfully, the party mood kept Theodora's tedious complaints at an ebb.

As two p.m. approached, the revelers departed to a variety of escort vessels. Matt and Sara cast off and left their slip for the last time and the first half-mile.

Chapter 7

A sweeping 'S' turn and a drawbridge in the Intercoastal Waterway were the only navigational challenges Matt faced before reaching the turning basin and harbor entrance. The channel was well marked with red and green buoys; shallow mud-banks on either side were plainly visible in the bright sunshine. The breeze carried the smells of fried food from several waterfront restaurants.

Matt stood on the stern deck, his right arm hooked over the boom, steering with his left foot. He had a clear view of other boat traffic, most of which was there to see them off. He was acutely aware that they were all watching his every move. After the 'S' turn, he saw the large clock on the bridge indicating another five minutes until it opened. Keeping a sharp eye on traffic, Matt held *TR*—his new nickname for the boat—in a circle pattern a hundred yards in front of the bridge. Sara waved at friends from the foredeck.

Thelma noticed it first, a feeling like heartburn deep in her chest. It was a familiar pain and she knew exactly what it was. Ever since the colonel had installed the new saltwater pump that fed her heat exchanger, her belt tended to slip. Unfortunately, unlike the colonel, Matt hadn't yet trained himself to scan her gauges on a regular basis and her temperature was rising at an alarming rate. She found the queen fanning herself on deck. "Feeling a bit warm, are we?"

"Too much dancing in the sun," Theodora said.

"You've got a lot to learn, Missy. That's our engine heating up and if we don't do something quick, we'll seize for sure. Come on, give us a hand with the rudder."

Matt kept one eye on the clock and the other on the dozen vessels in his entourage. One of his more rowdy friends swung his runabout in close and launched a barrage of water balloons. A fancy motor yacht close to eighty feet long appeared from around the bend and approached the bridge. Matt took his foot from the spoked wheel and moved to the other side of the cockpit for a clearer view of the waterway. He glanced astern and felt a touch of vertigo as the wheel spun out of control and *TR* made an abrupt turn to port.

He dove for the wheel.

A mud-bank loomed before the bow.

"Matt!" Sara shouted.

The wheel wouldn't budge.

Thelma held her breath as her keel split the mud. She came to a sucking stop. "There, that ought to get the boy's attention." She and the queen let go of the rudder.

Theodora pouted. "There goes my bottom paint."

"It's only mud," Thelma said. "I've spent half my life in a mud berth. Pickles the old timbers."

Gripped in a panic brought on by utter embarrassment, Matt shut the throttle and wrenched the shift lever into reverse. He goosed the engine. The RPMs jumped to 3000. "Please," he begged. Then he smelled it. His gaze dropped to the heat gauge. It was pegged in the red. He shut the engine down and collapsed back in the helmsman's seat, eyes closed. He remembered the colonel's warning. *Watch the gauges, her belt slips.*

Comments flew in over the stern, bruising his ego. "Makin' your own channel, eh Matt?"

"You're supposed to stay *between* the buoys."

"Great spot for a picnic, Matt."

The motor yacht gave five taunting hoots of its horn.

Laughter came from the walkway on the bridge.

"Way to go, Matthew," he muttered to himself.

Sara stepped into the cockpit. "What happened?"

Matt threw his hands up. "Don't know. I let go of the wheel for an instant...and bam. But look." He pointed to the heat gauge. "It's probably just as well. I might have burned up the engine."

The bell on the bridge sounded. Matt watched the bridge part and traffic pass through, then it closed. It wouldn't open for another half hour.

It took a humiliating ten minutes for Matt to adjust the tension on the belt. He fired up the engine and within minutes the temperature dropped. The mud was another thing. She was held fast and the backward thrust of the propeller wasn't enough to break the suction. A quick check of the tide tables told him he'd have a three-hour wait before the water would lift him free. He didn't think he could handle the ridicule.

A friend in a thirty-foot trawler offered to tow him off, but Matt didn't want to be even more conspicuous and obstruct traffic in the waterway. Instead, he let the mainsheet loose and he and Sara pushed the boom out until it was at a right angle to the hull. Then he hailed the smallest of his escorts, a ski boat with six people aboard. "If four of you hang on the end of the boom, we might be able to rock her out."

In seconds, his buddies dangled like gorillas from the boom's end and *TR* took on a list to port. Matt gave the engine maximum revs. "Come on, sweetie," he urged.

"Here we go," cried Thelma. "Our Matt's a clever boy."

The mud let loose, and with a slurp, *TR* eased back into the channel.

Applause broke out from the surrounding boats and cheers sounded from the bridge.

Humbled beyond care, Matt resumed his circle pattern. He slid an arm around Sara's waist. "Well, Babe, this first half mile can be a real bitch."

The bridge finally opened and *TR* passed into the turning basin. Matt headed her bow to the wind and Sara hoisted the mainsail. They motor-sailed beyond the protection of the breakwater and met the Atlantic swells. *TR*'s bluff bow shouldered aside the waves in a burst of spray and her deck rolled to a rhythm born off the coast of Africa. With a final blast of horns and whistles, the escorts waved farewell and turned back.

As soon as *TR* cleared the spoil area north of the channel, Matt and Sara set the working jib and staysail. Matt cut the engine and sighed at the momentary silence. The whispers and laughter of water and wind soon filled the void. He felt *TR* come alive, the power of the wind coursing through her sails and into her hull. She surged forward, free from the shackles of land. The wind held steady from the south-southeast and she reached off into the Gulf Stream.

Thelma clasped her hands to her chest. "Oh, glory, Missy, don't this just shiver your timbers."

"Shiver my...? God, you sound like a parrot. But yeah, it feels good to have my sails up. I've even got a shade of red nail polish to match them." She fluffed her black hair. "A bit of henna will be the crowning touch."

Thelma gave an impatient huff. "This is no Easter parade on the Thames, Missy. You'd best pay attention to chafe on our lines and the set of the sails. And who knows what adjustments your precious new rigging will need. Our captain is a bit green yet and we have to watch out for ourselves."

Chapter 8

Nautical twilight, that magic time when the first stars appear and the horizon still holds a sharp edge, brought a slight chill. Matt shrugged into a sweater and poured himself a cup of hot coffee from a thermos. Leftover egg salad sandwiches would do for dinner. The wind had picked up, filling the tanbark sails with a powerful ration of fresh sea air. The press of wind kept *TR* heeled fifteen degrees to port and there was urgency to the sound of the water churning along her hull.

Sara sat curled in the protection of the canvas spray dodger that covered the main hatch and forward area of the cockpit. Her eyes were closed, head cradled in crossed arms. Occasionally, a haunting moan, like a distant foghorn, rose from her huddled form. Two hours before she had given up her lunch to Poseidon and now, when the waves of nausea peaked, there was nothing left but dry heaves.

"Useless baggage," Theodora said in disgust. "Just what Matt needs, a high-maintenance first mate."

"Hold your tongue, Missy. She'll get her sea legs in time."

"Yeah, well let's hope it's a short time. I'm damn tired of her spewing on my decks."

"Could be worse," Thelma said. "It didn't take Matt long to balance our sails. Mind you, I'm still not happy with the set of our jib, but we've got an easy helm now and he won't have to work to keep us on course."

"And what about our anchor?" The Queen asked. "It's still loose in the chocks and beyond my power to fix it. I shudder to think what I'll look like in the morning if Matt doesn't get it secure. It already put a six-inch gash in my sheer strake."

A wave slapped hard against the hull and Matt ducked under the dodger to avoid getting drenched. Sara moaned.

Matt sat beside her and stroked the back of her head. "By morning the seas should quiet down. Why don't you go below...try to sleep."

When Sara spoke it was a whimper. "What about you?"

He laughed. "I'm so hyped about starting this trip I'll be awake for the next three days."

Sara gave a weak nod.

Funny, being seasick never crossed my mind. He remembered a time as a teenager when he did get seasick on a friend's fishing boat. It was the pits and he felt sorry for Sara.

TR lurched over a wave and buried her bow in the trough. The anchor clanged against the bowsprit. Matt buckled on a safety harness, then crept forward. The bow pitched like a crazed elevator. He clipped the harness onto the lifeline then wrestled the sixty-pound plow anchor back into its chocks. He retied the lashings and added an extra one for good measure. *These tie-downs are useless in a seaway. I'll have to rig a pin to hold this sucker in place.*

TR rode an invisible roller coaster as the sea disappeared in the night. A sliver of moon shone in the east and a steady drone of wind played in her rigging. The only light, a faint red glow, came from the compass mounted on the binnacle in front of the wheel. Alone in the cockpit, Matt watched the pale pink compass card swing hypnotically from east to northeast and back again. He kept a light hand on the wheel, making minor adjustments when a wave pushed the bow off course.

He chose a bright star off the starboard bow as a guide. Images of ancient navigators and future space travelers invoked an infinite sense of freedom. There was no place he couldn't go. All he had to do was follow the wind. He grinned in the darkness.

Many of his friends hadn't understood how he could give it all up—the house, the business, the mod-cons. "You've got it made," they said. "You're on easy street. Why take a risk like going to sea?"

Standing on the stern deck, one hand on the backstay, the rush of wind in his face, he looked at the heavens, then back toward Florida. "This is why!" he shouted. His laughter carried to the stars.

He needed challenge in his life. For him, easy street was a bore. The first years of building a business satisfied that need, but when it became routine, restlessness set in. He hankered to see the world, but the Navy held no appeal. His own boat, his own agenda and a test of his own self-reliance at the whims of Mother Nature made cruising the obvious choice.

Thelma smiled fondly at the boy. *Just like my first owner. A man destined for the sea.* Since the breeze had picked up, a heavy, bloated sensation told her she was due for a reef in her mainsail. It was bellied out in a stiff arc and the stronger gusts felt like bouts of gas. She loosened the belt at her waist.

Lounging on the forward bunk, Theodora burped. "God, I feel like I've eaten a whole glazed pig. If we don't shorten sail soon, I swear I'll have stretch marks."

Thelma reached over from the chain locker and pinched the queen's waist.

She slapped her hand away.

"Gracious, Missy, you've nothing to fear, your skin's as soft as chamois. Our Matt needs to know how far he can push us, and we aren't near to bursting a seam."

At that moment, *TR* fell off a steep wave, tilted thirty degrees and landed hard on her beam. The lockers above the settee where Sara lay sleeping flew open. Canned goods, baking supplies and packets of rice tumbled down. She instinctively held up one arm and rolled to the side.

Matt heard a clatter of cans, a yelp and loud thump when she hit the floor. *Jesus! Now what?*

Thelma scowled at the queen. "I don't suppose *you* know how the clips securing those lockers came to be loose?"

Theodora fluffed her pillow and yawned. "Haven't a clue."

Matt stuck his head in the companionway. In the dim light he could see Sara struggling to sit up amid the scattered stores. "You okay?"

She picked up a can of tuna and threw it against the bulkhead. It bounced off the settee and plunked on the floor. "No! I'm not okay," rubbing her forehead.

He climbed down and knelt beside her. "What's wrong?"

"What's wrong? I feel like shit and there's another lump on my head. This isn't my idea of a pleasure cruise, in fact, right now a house in suburbia sounds like paradise."

Matt took her hand and kissed her brow. "Look, you're a little seasick is all. Happens to most everyone. You'll get over it."

"I'll never eat egg salad again."

"It won't be on the menu." He helped her to her feet. "Give me a hand putting a reef in the main. Won't take long, then I'll come down and straighten the mess out."

She gave him a weary nod. She slipped on her foul weather coat and they climbed to the cockpit.

The wind had shifted into the south. Matt checked his watch, 3 a.m. "The cold front's on its way. How soon it gets here depends on how fast the wind clocks around to the west. My guess is we have about six hours."

"And then?" Sara asked.

"It'll blow like stink from the north. Hopefully we'll be tucked behind some little cay in the Abacos."

She hunched her shoulders and sat in the helmsman's seat. "Where are we now?"

"I haven't worked up a fix yet, but we should be on the banks by daybreak."

"Let's do this reef thing. I'm about ready to lose it again."

"Sheet in the main, steer downwind and keep the wind over your right shoulder," Matt told her. He picked his way to the mast, careful to always have a grip on something solid. He'd been through the reefing process a number of times at the dock. The colonel had rigged a simple system of lines so the mainsail could be reduced from one position at the mast.

Like an old hand, Matt dropped the main, hooked in the first reef point and winched in the clew-line to tighten the foot. Then he hoisted the now smaller sail and headed back to the cockpit. The wind carried the sound of Sara retching.

Thelma clucked with sympathy. She felt badly for Sara, doubled over in the cockpit. But at the same time, she worried that the poor dear had steered off course. The wind now came straight over her stern, threatening to jibe her main. She noticed Sara hadn't secured the main sheet, and Thelma knew only to well the damage her boom could do if it swung out of control.

Chapter 9

TR swung farther off course. Matt felt the shift in wind. As he stepped into the cockpit, the mainsail shuddered, then backfilled with a snap.

Like the twitch of a shark's tail, the boom shot across the cockpit and struck Matt in the chest. He locked his arms around the end. Sara screamed as line shrieked through the blocks and the boom swept the deck. Thelma, who now shared her limited worldly powers with the queen, managed to kink the sheet-line. It jammed in the block.

Matt dangled three feet over the sea. "Haul me in," he gasped.

Sara reached for the line and hauled like a madwoman.

As soon as his feet touched the deck, Matt scrambled into the cockpit.

Theodora looked up from her mirror. "What's the ruckus?"

Thelma shook her head, amazed. "Lord, Missy, where have you been?"

"Checking for stretch marks, but I'm okay."

Thelma was livid, her voice rose. "Our captain came within a tarred seam of dining with Davy Jones while you were lost in that mirror again. If you knew what was good for you, you'd deep-six the bloody thing!"

Sara's face was white as sea foam. She stared, slack-jawed, then blinked. "I don't believe what just happened."

Matt rubbed the sore spot on his sternum and rolled the stiffness out of his right shoulder. "I do." He reached out, took the sheet-line from Sara, snugged the boom in tight and then spun the wheel. TR swung to starboard and crossed the wind. In a controlled jibe, the main shifted to port and they resumed their easterly course.

Sara curled up under the dodger. "I'm really out of it. I thought I had that line cleated off... I'm so sorry."

"Jesus, Sara. What if I'd been knocked cold and gone in the drink? What would you have done?"

"I ... I don't know."

"Exactly, and that's my fault. I've let you slide by with hardly any working knowledge of the boat. We have to change that, run some man overboard drills and stuff. It's too easy to get overconfident when things go well. We should never forget about Mr. Murphy." He pointed to the self-steering apparatus mounted on the stern. "The colonel told me how that vane works, but I didn't think we'd need it for such a short trip. I'll hook it up in the Bahamas, give us a break from steering."

"Maybe by then I won't be puking my guts out. I'm feeling a little better. I think that episode scared the *Mal de Mer* right out of me."

"Take the wheel, then. I'll check the GPS and see how far we are from the banks." Below, Matt gathered the spilled stores and dumped them in the galley sink for the time being. Then he checked the screen on the Global Positioning System he had mounted over the chart table. Days before, after purchasing the GPS unit from West Marine, he'd entered the necessary waypoints that would guide him safely across the Bahama Banks. The unit told him his course, speed and distance remaining.

Theodora watched him mark their position on the chart. "I wish he'd bought a GPS with one of those fancy high-tech antennas for my mast," she said.

"Humph," Thelma replied. "Just more to go wrong, Missy. All that frivolous gear makes a captain slave to his ship."

Theodora frowned into her mirror, then plucked an eyebrow. "So what's wrong with that? I used to own slaves."

"I can imagine," Thelma said, "but I was built for the sea, not to be some...some marina Madonna."

Matt climbed back to the cockpit. "Fifteen miles from the banks. Another twenty to a good anchorage."

Sara looked over her left shoulder and scanned the night sky. "Will we beat the front?"

He held his hand to the wind. It was still in the south. "Maybe."

White sand on the Little Bahama Bank reflected the sun's rays, turning the shallow water a surreal aquamarine. The aroma of fresh brewed coffee wafted through the cockpit and Matt's stomach grumbled. He stood behind the wheel stretching sideways at the waist to ease the morning stiffness. His Polarized sunglasses cut the sun's glare, easing the strain on his blue eyes. The brim of a floppy canvas hat shaded his nose.

They had reached the bank two hours before. The wind had backed to the west and the sea treated them to a gentle swell. The sails were set wing-on-wing—the main to port and the genoa held to starboard with a long spruce pole. They ghosted eastward like a giant bird in a delicate following breeze.

Sara appeared in the companionway with a steamy cup of coffee. She handed it up to Matt, then climbed into the cockpit and kissed his cheek. "It's so quiet below, for a minute I thought we were back in the marina."

They were both down to shorts, T-shirts and sunblock. "You must be feeling better."

Her smile rivaled the sun. "Like new. Last night is already a distant memory." She sat in the shade of the dodger. "Hard to imagine we're in for bad weather."

Matt pointed to the northwest where a dark ridge of clouds had crept over the horizon. "There's our cold front. I listened to the forecast earlier. They predict winds to forty knots and temperatures in the fifties."

She gave a mock shiver. "Bummer."

Theodora lay face down on her lead ballast, knees bent, slender ankles crossed. She watched the sand and conch-grass slide by six feet under her keel. A four-foot stingray fluttered out of the sand. Occasionally a dark head of coral would drift ominously by in the blue haze. "Shouldn't we be worried about hitting coral? I can just feel my stem slamming into one of those mega-chunks."

Thelma paused from picking dust balls off her slippers. "Matt can see those heads readily enough in this light. I'm sure he has the sense not to sail these waters in the dark. Mind you, I wish Sara would keep watch from our bow, the set of our sails makes it hard to see well ahead."

"She's more interested in Matt than me," the queen said. "He got coffee and a kiss and there's still a little of her vomit on my deck."

"No worse than bloody fish guts," Thelma said. "A good douse with a bucket of sea water will take care of it."

"That's my point. Where's the bucket of water?"

An hour later, Matt picked out the distant smudge of a cay off the port bow. The wall of clouds in the northwest reached halfway up the sky. He felt a cool breath on his neck. "Let's get these sails down. I'll feel better with a double reefed main and the staysail."

By the time he and Sara finished with the sail change, a distinct green wisp of casuarina trees showed on the cay. Matt nodded forward. "Our anchorage." He glanced over his shoulder. A dark, cigar-shaped cloud like the crest of a gigantic wave loomed above. "It'll be close. Get your foul weather gear on."

Twenty minutes later the west wind died. A strip of white sand lined the cay like a taunting grin. TR's sails drooped in the pregnant air.

"Hang on, Missy," Thelma said. "It's gettin' on to blow."

The hiss of driven rain grew like rising static in God's radio. A paw of frigid air shot from the squall line. *TR's* sails billowed with a crack. Her hull shuddered and she heeled with the impact, then surged forward with a bone in her teeth.

Sara watched with platter eyes from the companionway. Rain slashed at the back of Matt's jacket. A soprano wind sang in the rigging. He glanced at the compass and took a bearing on the cay as it vanished behind the gray curtain of the squall.

Chapter 10

"I can't see shit! Get on the bow!" Matt yelled over the deafening deluge.

Sara scrambled forward and took up watch at the bow pulpit. Thelma pursed her lips in disapproval of the scene. Eight knots in shallow, coral seas with land dead ahead and poor visibility–not what she would call a sensible thing to do. "Come with me, Missy. She led the queen aft. "Our boy seems to think he can't anchor without a safe harbor, but all we really need is shallow water. You release the staysail sheet and I'll tend the anchor."

Theodora balked at the order. "Just one min..."

"This is no time to argue," Thelma snapped. "Do as I say."

Thelma's tone shocked the queen into submission.

Matt felt a jolt, then heard the staysail begin to flog. Its sheet line snaked out of the cockpit. Sara fumbled with the halyard then hauled the sail down. TR's speed dropped to six knots.

The lashings on the anchor proved no problem for Thelma, but to launch the beast from its chocks would take more than she and the queen could muster. It was up to Matt or Sara, but first she had to make them aware.

The high-pitched tweet of the depth sounder alarm caught Matt's attention. He saw the flashing red light and realized there was only three feet of water under the keel...now two. He looked ahead. The darkness wasn't just heavy rain; there were trees. He spun the wheel hard to port. "Anchor!" he yelled and gave Sara a thumbs down. She immediately bent to the task.

TR rounded into the gale, her mainsail whipped to a mad chatter. Wind and rain roared over her bow like a solid wave. She slowed to a stop. Matt heard the rattle of chain, slow at first then faster as TR's bow swung in the wind and the chain ran out. He trotted forward and stooped to help Sara set the brake on the windlass. The chain went taut. TR jerked on her tether, reared back and set her anchor. Matt gave Sara's shoulder a squeeze. "Nice work, let's pray it holds."

Matt released the main halyard and clawed the sail down. The wind had kicked up a two-foot chop. *TR* bucked at her anchor while he and Sara fought billowing canvas and lashed the sails in place. Afterward, they huddled in the cockpit under the canvas dodger and waited for the squall to pass.

"I'm anxious to know where we are," Matt said.

"I'm glad you thought of the anchor, there's coral everywhere."

"It's damn strange. The alarm on the depth-sounder is what clued me in to dropping the anchor, but I know I turned it off."

Sara wiped the face of the instrument where it showed behind an open port. "Maybe the rain shorted something. A lot of water blew under the dodger before we turned into the wind."

Matt fiddled with the alarm switch and the sensitivity knob. The alarm chirped. He shrugged. "Seems to be working okay."

The rain let up and the cay emerged a scant quarter mile away. Green foliage of casuarinas and palmetto palms gave false substance to the low, sandy crescent.

"Yeow!" Matt jumped to his feet. "I had no idea we were that close. We must have been flying."

Sara climbed to the stern deck and scanned the water. She crooked a finger at Matt. "Have a look."

He stood beside her and looked down. A jagged cluster of antler coral threatened to make driftwood of *TR's* rudder. The sight made him catch his breath. "Jeeze, good thing the anchor held. Now that we can see what we're doing, Let's get our butts outta here."

He started the diesel and motored slowly forward while Sara winched in the chain. The wind toyed with *TR's* bow, causing Matt to steer a zigzag course to the anchor. Sara gave him a thumbs up, then pointed to port. He put the helm over.

"No!" Sara yelled and frantically tried to wave him off.

TR's keel thumped against something hard enough to be felt on deck.

Theodora cringed then shook her fist at Sara. "Look what you've done, you miserable minx."

Matt shifted into reverse. "What the hell are you doing?" he shouted. *TR* bumped once more.

Sara rushed to the cockpit. "I was pointing at the coral."

"Get back up there and point where it's safe to go."

Christ, Matt thought. What was she thinking? They'd been over this before. He followed her directions through the coral maze and finally reached the south end of the cay.

A shallow spit of milky sand ended with a deep blue slash that clearly marked the passage to the island's leeward side. Once they rounded the corner, the sea flattened and the wind dropped by half. The tall wispy plumes of the casuarina pines dipped and swayed in an exotic fan dance. They were alone in the anchorage. A sweeping curved beach beckoned with welcoming arms.

Thelma plunked down on the starboard fuel tank and fanned herself. "Any closer and we'd have been a beach-front condo, Missy. You'd best be thankful Sara is handy with our anchor." Theodora paced the bilge. Her manicured nails looked like ragged flakes of thick varnish and her hair a snarled mass of twine. "Thankful hell, I'd like to ring her neck. If she'd been the lookout on my royal barge, I'd have had her head."

"If you're wanting to place blame, it always lies with the captain," Thelma said. "I suspect the next time our Matt is faced with a similar situation, we'll see the anchor down in a timely fashion."

"How can you just sit there like nothing happened? We could have ended our days on that beach or some miserable chunk of coral!"

Thelma winked at the queen. "So where's the disaster? What-ifs don't count and we only lost a small chip of paint off our lead. To look at you one would think we all but sank. I save my gray hairs for times when the barnacles abandon ship."

They anchored a hundred yards from shore in a clear patch of white sand. Matt stripped to his skivvies. Shivering from the cold, he grabbed a mask and snorkel from the dive locker. "I'll check the damage. Why don't you rustle us up some grub?"

"Sorry about the screw up," Sara said.

"So am I. Can't have many of those. We'll work on it." He jumped into the crystal waters. It was cool, but not icy. A quick look told him the lead keel had lost a bit of paint–no big deal.

Drying off, he told Sara, "We got off lucky this time. Just remember, you're my eyes when you're on the bow. I'll go wherever you point."

Sara gave him a weak smile. "I can safely say I'll never make that mistake again."

Theodora sneered at Sara's remark. "It's the ones she does make that worry me."

An hour later, after lines were coiled, sail covers on and gear stowed, a stack of pancakes adorned the dining table. Matt dug in with abandon. "Mmmm, these are great, Babe. Best meal I've had in years."

Sara poked a fork at the lone flapjack on her plate. "Wish I could say the same. My stomach's still not ready for this. I probably lost ten pounds last night."

Matt poured another dollop of syrup on his mound of cakes. "Hey, I've got it. We start a weight loss charter service—guaranteed ten pounds a day or we pay for the groceries. How's that sound?"

"I refuse to endorse it. No one wants to feel as sick as I was—even for twenty pounds a day."

"Yeah, it was probably a one time deal."

"If it wasn't, I'm outta here."

Theodora perked up. "Hear that? Things are looking up."

"Heartless," Thelma mumbled.

"Are you serious?" Matt asked.

Sara reached across the table and rested a hand on Matt's forearm. "Don't take it personally, but yes, I'm absolutely serious. If extreme nausea is all I have to look forward to whenever we go to sea, what's the sense?"

Matt sat back and thought a moment. "I see your point. But let's give it a fair trial, okay? Maybe try some medication like those ear patches."

"Easy for you to say. I hate taking drugs."

"Hey, come on, we're talking a life together. Isn't that worth toughing it out for a while?"

"If we're talking a life together, would you consider returning to Florida with me if I don't get over being seasick?"

"Then *I'd* be miserable...I mean...I set out to see the real world, not Disney World."

Sara shoved her plate aside. "I guess you're taking the advice of your guru, Zeke, to heart."

"Guru? What's Zeke got to do with it, anyway?"

"I heard you guys talking one morning. Zeke was delivering his usual nautical gems and then he asked about me. You told him I still hadn't made up my mind about joining you. Then he says," she mimicked Zeke's raspy voice. "'Listen son, all you gotta remember is there's plenty of women out there, but a good boat is really hard to find.' Then the two of you busted a gut laughing."

Matt stuck his fork into the pile of pancakes and left it like a lone arrow. "Jeeze, Sara, that was just some male ego humor, not one of life's lessons. But you're right, I never made it a secret I would go with or without you."

"So it's a life together on your terms."

"Well, yeah, for this stage of it, anyway."

Sara moved to the other side of the table and sat hip to hip with Matt. "I knew that when I came along, but I have the right to wish for something else."

"Sure you do," Matt said. "But don't plan on me changing my mind about sailing the world."

She gave a curt nod. "Fair enough."

He cleared the table and cleaned up in trade for Sara's cooking. "What do you say we go ashore and stretch our legs?"

"You're not thinking of swimming, are you?" Sara asked. "It's frigid out there."

"No. I'd like to try out the new dinghy. I have yet to inflate it and it needs christening."

They slipped on their jackets and climbed topside. The wind had a bite to it and carried the scent of land, a rich blend of earth, trees and tide. The aggressive rumble of surf sounded like a drum corps practicing on the windward side of the small cay.

Matt took the foot-pump from a cockpit locker then untied the collapsed dinghy and oars from where they were lashed on the coach roof behind the mast. Sara helped him unfold the gray neoprene bundle on the foredeck. Matt attached the pump and stomped on the wooden bellows. As the air hissed in, the flattened mass began to grow.

When the dinghy was half inflated, Sara started to laugh.

"What's so funny?" Matt asked between stomps.

"It reminds me of some old pork sausage links I once found in my parents fridge."

"So how about we name it Porky?"

She clapped her hands. "Perfect. I love it." She went below and returned with a black marker pen. When the dinghy was full to bursting, she handed the pen to Matt. "You do the honors."

The pen squeaked as Matt printed PORKY in thick block letters.

Thelma was the first to notice the growing apparition that sat on the forward hatch. "Oh ho, Missy. I believe we've got company."

Chapter 11

He appeared to be a strapping young lad, and even though he was seated on the hatch cover, Thelma could tell he'd stand well over six feet. Curly brown hair ringed a cherubic face and he wore a short-sleeved shirt with wide, horizontal red and white stripes that stretched on his torso as if he were over-inflated. His sunburned midriff showed above baggy Madras shorts that blazed in hues of yellow and green so bright they could burn off fog. A pair of high-top black tennis shoes looked as if they'd grown on his feet.

When Matt finished the Y on *PORKY*, the new spirit lost his translucent qualities and Thelma saw the rosiness in his cheeks and the soft brown eyes of a seal pup. She sighed. "Isn't he a doll?"

Below where Matt had written PORKY, he lettered in TT - TR. Then sat back to admire his handiwork. *"Porky*, tender to *TR."*

Sara smiled. "Sweet."

Theodora came up behind Thelma. "Bet he eats like a whale."

"He belongs with our new tender," Thelma said. "Keep a civil tongue and give the boy a break."

Theodora held two fingers to her mouth and let rip a piercing whistle. "Hey, you with the lighthouse for trousers."

Porky looked confused until he spotted Theodora waving at him from the main cabin. He pointed a finger at his chest. "Me?"

Under her breath, the queen said, "No, the other court jester."

Thelma gave her a sharp elbow. "Yes dear, you! Come on down for a little chat." To Theodora she said, "Be nice."

Porky hung one buttock over the side of the hatch then made a clumsy leap to the cabin sole. He stumbled to one knee but managed to come to his feet in front of Thelma. He held out his hand. "Hi, I'm Porky."

Thelma took his hand in both of hers. "Welcome aboard, dear, I'm Thelma. Don't let the queen here tie you in knots."

Porky's eyes widened as he looked at Theodora. "A real queen?"

Theodora pulled her shoulders back, tucked in her chin and held out a limp hand. "Queen Theodora Regina of Rome."

Porky grabbed the proffered hand and pumped it with wild enthusiasm. "Gosh...a real queen." He kept pumping away until Theodora jerked her hand loose.

On deck, Matt tied a short painter to Porky's bow, then lifted. "Let's toss it in and see how it works."

Sara took hold of the stern. "On three."

Porky snapped to attention. "Oops, gotta go." He leapt to his dinghy just as Matt and Sara tossed it over the side.

"What a sweetie," Thelma said.

Theodora pinched the bridge of her nose and shook her head. "He's old enough to be my brother, but something tells me he's not cruising with a full suit of sails."

Thelma watched Matt and Sara climb into *Porky*. "Could be he's just shy, Missy. Mind you, he doesn't put on airs like some I know." She arched an eyebrow and peered at the queen. "But it's that what makes him adorable."

Matt fitted the aluminum oars into the thick rubber oarlocks. "Cast off." Sara pushed them clear of *TR* and Matt pulled hard on the oars. His stroke wasn't balanced and with no keel in the dinghy's fabric floor to help it track, Matt rowed a squirrelly course toward shore, laughing at his efforts. "Boy, can you tell I need practice?"

"You think this is funny," Sara said. "Wait'll you see me try and row this tub."

The wind didn't help. Each time Matt tried to rest at the oars, they'd be blown backwards.

Porky sat at the bow on the stubby pontoon, dangling his feet in the water. He liked having wet feet; it made his sneakers soft. He bounced on his air-filled seat like someone testing a mattress, then grinned. It was the first time he'd ever been an inflatable boat and he was used to people calling him a tub.

He long ago accepted his lot in life. He knew he'd have to be satisfied with small skiffs, bass boats and the like, though he'd once made it to a shrimp trawler. Unfortunately, that boat had gone down in Hurricane Camille. Over the years, he'd come to realize that nobody ever named a fancy yacht or a real ship *Porky*.

But today, he was proud. Tender to a queen, he thought. Queen Theodora of Rome. Now that was something he and the queen had in common. For years he'd been an aluminum skiff in Rome. True, he'd spent most of the time on a trailer in his owner's garage, but he usually got out on weekends for fishing trips on the lakes in northern Georgia.

And the old lady, Thelma; he liked her accent. She wasn't from Rome or any other place he could recall. He wondered what she meant by the queen tying him in knots. He hoped it was a bowline–that was his favorite.

By the time Matt reached shore, his arms ached and he'd worked up a sweat even in the cold wind. He and Sara scrambled out when the bow touched sand, then hauled *Porky* high on the beach. "This is good enough," Matt huffed.

Sara held up the painter. "Shouldn't we tie this to something?"

He waved his hand in dismissal. "Nah, we're way above the tide line."

She shrugged and dropped it in the sand.

Matt took off at a trot down the beach, as much to stretch his legs as to explore their first deserted, almost-tropic isle.

Porky always felt insecure when left unattended without his painter attached to something solid. He watched Sara bend and pick up a cowrie shell and hoped she'd stay close. But no, she wandered off with never a backward glance.

Ten minutes later a fortified gust of wind reached under Porky's bow and ripped him off the sand. He did a double back flip, landing right side up in the water, twenty feet from shore.

Chapter 12

Tight in the wind's grip, *Porky* sailed into the bay. "I knew it!" he shouted, looking frantically toward shore, but Matt and Sara were nowhere to be seen. A hundred yards out, *TR* sat placidly at anchor–his only hope for salvation. If he missed her there was only the endless ocean beyond.

Thelma and the queen were on the bow. He watched Thelma slide down her anchor chain. As he drifted closer, he heard her yell, "Throw me your painter. I'll make it fast."

His power over worldly things had never been very strong. Near panic, he tried to manipulate the thin nylon line. He wailed when his first attempt to gather the line flopped back in the water.

"Let him go," the queen said. "Our next tender might be one of those slick fiberglass jobs with an outboard."

Thelma had come to expect such snobbish remarks from Theodora, and ignored her. This was no time for a joust. She could see the distress on Porky's face. He looked as if he were about to cry. "Steady now, steady as she goes," she said.

Her voice soothed him like oil on rough seas. He finally managed a clumsy coil, but he sailed wide of Thelma's outstretched hand. Then a maverick gust spun his bow her way. He cast the line with all his strength. It was a pitiful throw at best, but Thelma snagged the bitter end. She whipped a clove-hitch onto her anchor chain and *Porky* snuggled alongside her hull.

When Matt and Sara returned to where they'd left the dinghy, all they found were their footprints.

He scanned the anchorage. "Where the...?"

Sara's arm shot out, pointing at *TR*. "There, it's alongside the boat."

"Shit! I wonder if someone's aboard." He studied the sand then shook his head. "No other footprints. Must have blown off the beach."

For the second time that day, Matt went for a chilly swim. The dinghy painter had somehow knotted on the anchor chain; he could hardly believe their luck. He rowed to the beach to pick up Sara, vowing to always secure the dinghy.

When they were back aboard *TR*, Matt bundled up in an outfit of soft synthetic fleece and fixed them both cups of hot tea. Nestled into a corner of the settee he warmed both hands on a chipped mug with the caption *Wood floats*. He was still puzzled over *Porky* and grateful that Sara hadn't hounded him with I-told-you-so's for not securing the painter. "Can you imagine what the odds were of the dinghy painter knotting itself on the anchor chain?" Matt asked.

Sara had decided to tackle Michener's book, *Caribbean,* and sat at the table, legs curled under. She looked up from the pages. "Too bad we weren't playing the Florida lottery."

"Really, it wouldn't happen again in a lifetime. I reckon we've used up a year's worth of good dingy karma."

Thelma chuckled over the exchange.

"I wish a little of that would brush off on me." She grimaced and rubbed her shin. "I caught a toe on a coiled line and whanged myself on a winch when I climbed aboard just now."

"What is it with you and bruises? I swear you've got a new one every day."

"I don't know. It's not like I'm accident-prone. I was sure I'd stepped well clear of that rope. Sometimes I think this boat has it in for me."

He laughed. "Right. Next you'll tell me you think the queen is jealous."

She lowered her head and turned a page, a curtain of blond hair hiding her profile. "It crossed my mind," she mumbled.

Thelma, eavesdropping from the chain locker wanted to reach out and give Sara a hug. *If you only knew the half of it, dear girl.*

Theodora dropped in from the forward hatch. "Took her long enough. I was beginning to think barked shins and a few goose eggs were too subtle."

Thelma crossed her arms and cocked her head in frank appraisal of the queen. "If I didn't know better, I'd think your soul was riddled with dry rot. You treat Sara like a Jonah. You'd leave Porky adrift in mid-Atlantic and you'd love to see me walk the plank. A ship is a small world, Missy; you're bound to whistle up a storm."

Theodora arched her brows and looked down her nose at Thelma. "If that's what it takes to get rid of the riffraff, fine. I didn't get where I am by accepting second best."

"We're second best, are we?"

"Hardly. That Porky is nothing but honorable mention all the way. And you, look at yourself."

Thelma looked down the front of her robe and made a slight adjustment to the belt.

The queen carried on. "A worn out frump with no self respect. With that head full of curlers you look like a boiler room. You're fathoms from second best."

The attack left Thelma speechless. She'd never been spoken to in such a way. There was a sting to the queen's words that rivaled the barbed tail of a ray. Thelma's sense of self was as stout as her keel timber, but the lash of the queen's tongue had definitely rattled her rigging. She sniffed, then tidied the cuffs on her robe. "Who are you to judge, Missy? There's some wouldn't tolerate the likes of you. And as for self respect, I learned before my bronze turned green that my mission wasn't to impress others."

"Well, don't expect me to be content with what I've got. I won't apologize for my ambition. Without it, I'd still be a bear-keeper's daughter, no better off than you or Porky."

Thelma considered herself better off than most, so she let the comment slide. But it was the first time she'd heard the queen speak of her childhood. "Bears you say? Real bears?"

"Yeah, he trained 'em to do silly tricks like stand on their front paws. Spent every minute with the mangy walking rugs, performing on street corners for spare change. The rest of our family could starve for the little he cared, but those effing bears never missed a meal."

Ahh, Thelma thought, the little queen has some punky wood in her keel after all. "Listen, Missy, just because I'm content with my lot, don't paint me like your father. I've ambition, too. It just happens I'm partial to the stately lines of my hull and don't give a hang for all those reverse transoms, fin keels and other techno-gobbledygook that can squeeze another knot out of the wind."

Theodora bent at the waist until her eyes were inches from Thelma's face. "That's exactly the attitude that kept my mother's table empty. I'll be damned if I sail in someone else's wake." She whirled and stomped off.

Thelma stared at the queen's rigid back, sighed, and pondered the heavy seas to come.

Chapter 13

Porky spent an uneasy night tethered to the sternrail of *TR*. Fortified gusts of wind caused him to tug violently on his painter. Memory of the day's near-catastrophe strained what little faith he had in the knot Matt used to secure him to the rail. He wished the captain had hoisted him on deck for the night so he could have relaxed and enjoyed a visit with Thelma and the queen.

By noon the next day, the northwesterly gale had dropped to a fresh breeze. The sun played coy behind high, thin veils of cirrus clouds. It was a favorable wind, so despite the cool temperatures, Matt decided to up-anchor and head east. He hauled the dinghy alongside then dragged it aboard for the next leg of the journey.

While Matt wrestled with his bulk, Porky stumbled around on deck. He caught sight of Thelma and beamed her a smile. Unfortunately for Porky, rather than lash the cumbersome inflatable to the cabin top, Matt opted to let out the air and fold it back up to keep the space clear.

Thelma had been on the verge of offering the chubby spirit a scone when Matt pulled the air-plug. The sudden whoosh made Porky jump. As the rush of air poured from his pontoons, he began to fade from view. He held up his hands in a helpless gesture, then gave Thelma a finger-wiggle wave. Matt knelt on the collapsed craft, squeezed out the last of the air, and Porky's brightly clad form vanished.

Matt lashed the dinghy in place then ducked below. Out of the wind, it was warm and quiet. The lingering aroma of coffee invited him to stay. He stood silently just inside the companionway until Sara looked up from her book. "You ready?" he asked.

She sighed, then nodded, dog-earing her page and set the book aside.

Matt ignored her lack of enthusiasm. She was probably still thinking about the trip over. "Here's the drill," he told her. "You're on the bow. Once the anchor is loose, I'll follow your directions through the coral. Remember, I go where you point."

She saluted. "Aye, aye, Sir."

"Hey, it'll be a nice sail. If we wait 'til the weather turns warm, the wind will be in the east and we'll have to beat the thirty miles to Green Turtle Cay."

She bundled into her coat, a hooded green behemoth that could probably double as a sea anchor. "I know, but I'd rather sit in this cozy cabin and read today."

"Yeah," Matt agreed, "it's a bit of a trade-off but your stomach will appreciate a smooth reach for five hours as opposed to a bouncy eight-hour beat. Let's not miss this wind."

She zipped up the coat, almost vanishing in its folds, and followed Matt into the cockpit. "You'd do well in sales."

Theodora hadn't been too keen on going to sea. She had counted on a couple of days in port to recuperate from the last bump and numerous near misses. As it was, it would be weeks before her nails grew back. When she had complained to Thelma, the old fart had laughed and said, "No reason to get your frames bent, Missy, we're at the mercy of the captain as much as he's at the mercy of the wind."

The queen was pleased to see Matt pry Sara from the comfort of her book. *If I have to suffer, so should she.* Theodora stationed herself half way up the mast, perched on the port spreader–close enough to observe the departure, but not close enough to frighten herself with another maze of coral to navigate.

Thelma stood before the mast, hands on hips, legs spread to accommodate the roll of her deck. Her daisy print robe, cinched tight at the waist, billowed in the wind and wispy gray locks streamed like kelp from her curlers. Nothing gave her more joy than going to sea.

As before, Matt's stomach had wound itself into a coiled snake over the first half-mile. He concentrated on one thing at a time, careful not to get ahead of himself. Once he'd started the engine, he kept an eye to the gauges. He followed Sara's arm signals, and within ten minutes they were out of the bay, clear of the coral and hoisting the sails.

The hiss and sizzle of water racing along her hull made Thelma want to dance. She hummed an old sea chantey and the swollen press of canvas almost made her swoon. She hailed the queen high in the spreaders. "Down we go, Missy, relax and enjoy. This is a fair-weather run. Time to get a whip on those frayed nerve-ends of yours."

Theodora leaned over, cupped the side of her mouth and yelled, "The only thing I'll whip is your ass if you don't quit with the flap."

Thelma chortled and skipped into a jig on the foredeck. The queen was such an easy catch.

Matt turned the helm over to Sara, then winched in the genoa sheet to quiet its light chatter. They'd been cruising at a good six knots for over an hour with an easy roll from a quartering sea. Matt had studied the charts and knew there was no coral to watch for in this area of the bank.

He pulled a life ring from the sternrail. "Okay, this is Carlos; he's a klutz." Matt heaved the yellow ring over the stern. "He just fell overboard. What are we going to do?"

Sara craned her neck and stared after the receding yellow dot.

"Watching him disappear is no help," Matt said. "If it was dark you wouldn't see him anyway."

She looked up at the sails. "So we stop the boat."

Matt pointed to the compass. "First get a reciprocal course. If our present course is less than 180, then add 180. If it's more than 180, subtract 180. Simple but important, otherwise we won't know where to look."

She glanced at the compass. "We're sailing east at 90. I add 180 and return on 270."

"Right. Now stop the boat."

She looked helplessly up at the bulging sails. "How?"

"Turn hard to port," Matt said.

She spun the wheel. *TR* swung into the wind. Her speed dropped. The sails set up a deafening clatter.

"Keep it hard over 'til she crosses the wind," Matt yelled.

TR's bow crossed the wind. The genoa stopped its tirade and backed into the rigging.

"Now put the helm over to starboard," Matt said, sheeting in the flapping mainsail.

Quiet descended. TR seemed stuck in the water. It was almost like being at anchor.

"I read about this in one of Eric Hiscock's books last night," Matt said. "It's called heaving-to. The main and rudder try to turn one way and the genoa tries to turn the other. The forces counteract each other and bingo, we're parked."

Sara shaded her eyes and looked back, trying to spot the yellow ring among the waves. "Do we sit and wait for Carlos to swim to the boat?"

Matt laughed. "Carlos can't swim, he's hanging onto the ring. We start the engine, then pull down the genoa and motor back on the reciprocal course."

They carried out the rest of the exercise, and in a matter of minutes, Matt spotted the yellow life ring on the face of a wave. *TR* plunged forward into the three-foot chop while Sara brought her alongside the ring.

Matt fished it out with a boat hook. "If Carlos were a real person, we'd throw him a life ring with a line attached and haul him aboard."

She clapped her hands. "Piece a cake."

He held up his index finger. "Not so fast. We're fooling around in ideal conditions. The truth is, if it's stormy or at night the chances of being rescued are odds against. The best policy is just don't fall over."

Sara had steered back to their easterly course. She lifted her hands from the wheel, palms up. "That's silly, how can you..."

He cut her off. "Think of this man overboard exercise as a shot in the dark, especially if no one sees you go over. Never forget the old maxim: One hand for you and one for the ship. That was the sole safety precaution aboard ships for centuries and it still holds true. Always hang on to something. The pitch of the deck is totally unpredictable." Thelma had watched the routine with an approving eye, silently applauding Matt for his wisdom about watching out for oneself. She looked askance at the queen. Unfortunately, the pitch of the deck wasn't the only thing that was totally unpredictable.

Chapter 14

Three languid weeks burbled by with the speed of a river barge against the tide. The low coral islands of the Abacos formed a secure barrier from the Atlantic swells and the subsequent flat seas made boat handling a breeze. Most stimulating were the native parrots whose raucous, penetrating screeches were the mental equivalent of stepping on a spiny urchin. Light, easterly winds brought warm air from the tropics. T-shirts and shorts replaced sweaters and long pants.

In deference to Sara's stomach, they only sailed on placid days. They cruised down the island chain with a course as random as they desired. Before anchoring for the night, Matt would cruise close to waterfront homes while Sara watched her laptop for a Wi-Fi hotspot. Most nights they could surf the web and e-mail friends and family from the boat. And Matt had to admit the internet access was a great tool when looking for information.

On longer passages he experimented with the wind-vane steering system, learning its quirks with the hope of making it a full-time member of the crew. When he felt confident it would hold a steady course he named it Fred, painting the name in bold red letters on the vane.

Matt's skills at eyeball navigation became sharper by the day. Soon, judging by the shades of aquamarine, umbers and greens, he could tell within a foot how deep the water was, or if coral, sand or grass lay below.

After practicing several more overboard drills, Matt surprised Sara one day by leaping off the stern. Her quick response at the helm left him with less than a hundred-yard swim to reach the stalled boat. He then feigned an injury so she had to winch him aboard. This was not something they had practiced. He remained mute, allowing her to solve the problem on her own. When she finally got him on deck he wrapped her in a congratulatory embrace.

Sara twisted from his arms. "What's to congratulate? It took me almost an hour to get you aboard."

Matt grabbed her wrist and pulled her back. "Lighten up on yourself. It's not me reaching the deck in record time that's important. It's you solving an unexpected problem entirely on your own. Next time it won't take so long and neither will anything else that comes out of the blue. Not much goes by the book out here and that's the only thing we can count on."

Amused, the queen had watched the entire exercise. "He'd be a corpse if the water was cold."

The intensity of earlier predicaments mellowed with sunshine and gentle seas. The idyllic sailing conditions created a sense of complacency in Matt. Soon, what was once high drama seemed a vague memory, as though recalled from a book read long ago.

Sara rarely put her book down and seemed disinterested in exploring the island culture, so Matt was often alone on his forays ashore. He poked into native boat-building shops and learned how local woods were used or chatted with island fisherman, picking up tricks of the trade. His appetite for any skill related to the cruising life was voracious—it was his approach to anything new. Back aboard, he'd share his adventures with Sara who listened with patience and amused interest in her eyes.

Eventually, Matt jerked the book from her hands. "Why don't you come ashore with me, see this stuff first hand? You can read that book anytime."

Sara snatched the book back. "I don't mind rowing in for fresh fruit or veggies, but my interest ends there. You sound like you're in school whenever you go ashore. The only way I'll make it through this trip is to look at it as a permanent vacation." She held up the book. "That means lots of this, maybe some swimming and diving and the occasional bit of sightseeing." She jammed a thumb in her chest. "I don't aspire to be a student of foreign culture. It's tough enough learning to sail."

"That's kind of limiting, wouldn't you say?"

"Hey," Sara said, "I'll be the first one to admit I have my limits and for now I've pretty much reached them. I'm not expecting you to follow suit. You do your thing, and let me do mine."

Matt tossed his hands up. "Okay, okay." He had assumed Sara would share his delight in experiencing the world beyond the U.S. He longed for a companion ashore, someone to share it all with. He assured himself that, in time, she'd grow bored with the "vacation" attitude. But in the mean time, he wasn't going to let her attitude spoil *his* party.

Seldom did they have an anchorage to themselves. Between the charter fleets and winter yachtsmen, it was often necessary for Matt to set two anchors to avoid swinging into a neighbor. Invariably, *TR,* with her varnished spars and sun-bleached bulwarks, would be the oldest, saltiest looking vessel in the crowd, eliciting constant inquiries about her age and history. Other sailors invited Matt and Sara aboard their respective yachts for coffee or sundowners. Matt, who enjoyed the camaraderie of the cruising community where landside social barriers were dissolved by the sea, was encouraged by Sara's willingness to attend and reciprocate. At least it was something they experienced together. Hopefully she'd begin to join him ashore.

Porky made a brief appearance aboard *TR* when he was reinflated at Green Turtle Cay. He knew his time with Thelma and the queen would be limited and bounded like a shore-leave sailor to where they sat drinking tea in the main cabin.

He gave them a two-handed wave. "I'm back!"

Theodora raised one arm and shied away as though he was sunshine and she had a hangover. "Look what the tide brought in," she muttered.

Thelma was delighted to see the boy and patted the cushion beside her. "Knot your painter and stay a while, lad. Don't pay the queen any mind." She handed Porky a cup and poured the tea.

"See that the Captain ties you off securely, now. We can't be worried about you going adrift again."

Porky slurped his tea and kept his gaze on the table. "I'm not so good with the knots, Thelma."

"Then it's time you learned," she said. She yanked off the rope at her waist and took him carefully through the bowline, clove hitch and square knot. She noticed the queen rolling her eyes and said. "It would spruce your rig to know these, too." The queen harumphed, but Thelma saw her eyes follow the moves.

A moment later, Matt lifted the dinghy to launch it over the side.

Porky took a hasty gulp of tea and leapt to his charge. Thelma snatched the falling cup.

Theodora was in her element. She adored the attention her classic looks attracted. Again, her hand mirror became a constant companion. She used a deeper shade of red on her recovering nails that matched the oxblood color of her main and genoa. Drenched in gardenia cologne, she paraded her decks with a critical eye for cosmetic blemishes on her woodwork. She correctly surmised that Sara had no intention of keeping up the varnish on her teak and praised Matt for touching up the chips and dings. Theodora was also convinced that Sara was not the right woman for her captain. To this end, she never missed a chance to trip the girl up or disrupt her routine. One of her favorite tricks was to release the latch on the fold-down counter in the galley whenever Sara was busy cooking. If the slab of maple didn't smack Sara's knuckles it would often thump her in the head when she bent down to close the oven door.

Thelma, who shared equally the influence over the ship, was powerless to stop the queen's juvenile antics. Furthermore, she argued with herself that possibly the queen was right and that they'd all be better off without Sara. This, of course, conflicted with her "live and let live" attitude and led her to question her ethics. *Perhaps I've been influenced by the mere presence of Theodora. After all, a shared berth is a new experience for me.*

Jealousy was out of Thelma's realm and she could no more comprehend the effects of that destructive emotion than she could the impact of the Eurodollar on the world economy.

Aside from her quandary over Sara and the queen, Thelma watched Matt with an appraising eye. The lazy days of sailing reminded her of the sweet times she had cruising the Hebrides under the command of her first owner. She was sure the man had possessed a sixth sense for the subtle set of a tide or the back-eddies near to shore. His navigation had been impeccable and he could sail her through a tight spot with a touch as slick as the varnish on her mast. His mastery of seamanship had left her with high expectations for anyone at her helm and these she applied to Matt.

Matt's efforts to balance her sails or set the anchor with proper scope frequently left her shaking her head in hopeless dismay.

However, she was impressed that he never hesitated to dive down and set the anchor by hand in questionable holding ground.

But Thelma's long experience also told her that when conditions were sweet as her bilge, it was sure as a compass reads north that any change would warrant a pucker.

Chapter 15

For Theodora, the sweet turned to sour that night. In her dreams, she lounged naked on embroidered silk pillows, drinking red wine. A massive Nubian eunuch with oiled, blue-black skin dressed in loincloth and turban fanned her body with ostrich plumes. As the slave's arm began to tire, the feathers swept close and tickled her midriff. That's when she woke up.

Thelma, roused by the queen's hysterical screams, spotted the company of roaches that scurried across the turn of her bilge. They produced an annoying sensation like tendrils of sargasso weed brushing against her hull. She'd been half expecting them ever since Matt had carted the boxes aboard. The warmer weather must have brought them out. They were mostly a nuisance, but the queen's fearful cries advanced them, in Thelma's mind, to near welcome guests. She found Theodora in the engine room, cowering on the engine block, white gown hitched up in two clenched fists, knees quaking. Her slender ankles shone like walrus ivory above black slippers. She stifled her screams when Thelma appeared, but her eyes had the wild cast of a timid swimmer in shark-infested waters.

"Do something!" she shrieked. "The little bastards are everywhere."

Thelma quelled a hearty laugh. "Only our captain can rid us of the carnivorous buggers. You'll be safe there for the night, Missy. Come dawn, they'll hole up in all our nooks and crannies and won't be a bother."

"I'm not staying up here all night!"

"Suit yourself, but they won't settle down until morning."

The queen's eyes turned to slits. Her knees stopped shaking. "Why is it they don't bother you?"

"Thelma stuck out one foot and wiggled it. "The fuzz on my slippers keeps 'em off like rat-guards on a hawser." She struggled to keep a straight face. What a hoot it would be to see the queen wear fuzzies.

"Rat-guards, hell," Theodora said. "They look like dead rats. The roaches will have me for lunch before I'd wear those."

Thelma turned her back on the queen to hide her grin. *Bon appetite.*

It was a calm night. An armada of cumulous clouds made a slow passage overhead. Wavelets burbled against Porky's neoprene hull. He'd been startled by the scream coming from his mother ship. His anxiety eased when the queen appeared on deck. He watched her slide his painter forward along her lifeline. Soon he was snug against her hull instead of tailing behind. The solid contact with his mother ship would allow him access to the vessel, but he hadn't thought of the queen or Thelma having the same privilege. He jerked back, astonished when the queen yelled, "Move your ass," and jumped, landing with a hollow thump on his inflated pontoon.

"Wel...welcome aboard, Your Maj...er...Your Highness." Never having hosted a royal visit, he wasn't sure what to do. He fumbled between a curtsy and a bow.

Theodora ignored him and glanced around the dinghy. "No cockroaches?" she asked.

That wasn't quite the response Porky had expected. "Cockroaches? You mean those little brown bugs?"

"Yes. My hull's infested with the little shits."

"Well, gosh, they're only bugs. What can they hurt?"

The queen shuddered. "The damn things are filthy and disgusting. How would you like having them crawl all over you?"

Porky scratched behind his ear and frowned. "They're not so bad. One time, when I was a wooden rowing skiff, I got eaten alive by carpenter ants. At least roaches don't eat wood."

Theodora smoothed out her gown and settled back with an air of presiding over her own domain. "You may have a point there. I'll stay 'til morning. Wake me at first light." She stretched out, exposing those ivory ankles, and closed her eyes.

Porky stared at the delicate shape of the queen's ankles rising to the fine curve of her calves. He fought a powerful urge to reach out and stroke them as an old memory came flooding back.

It was the year he'd shared a Hobi Cat on Lake Tahoe. His owners, fond of their nicknames, had named the starboard hull

Porky and the port hull *Tess.* Tess, the spirit, had been a spindly Irish teenager with luscious red hair brilliant as fire coral. She carried with her the lyrics of a thousand songs. She would lie on her back for hours, dangling her slender, bare feet in the crystal waters of the lake, singing tune after tune. Porky would sit on his starboard hull, just beyond reach of the enchanting young waif, humming along with the melodies. He became mesmerized by the flutter of white feet that danced like eelgrass in a surge whenever he and Tess were under sail. In fine weather they would be out sailing for hours and Tess' ankles would beckon like some diabolical fish lure. Driven half-mad with the desire to hold and caress the creamy appendages, Porky cried tears of frustration over the two yards that kept them away. He remembered an odd feeling of relief when the owners sold the catamaran and the new owners renamed the boat.

But now, not six inches away was a pair of ankles that rivaled those of Tess. He couldn't have been happier if they'd made him flagship of the U.S. Navy. Only inhibitions caused by Theodora's royal presence kept Porky's hands at bay. He wondered how soundly the queen slept.

The next morning, Matt poured a dollop of sweetened condensed milk into his coffee. His stomach coiled in protest when two brown roach carcasses plopped into the java. Still in a mild morning stupor, he calmly stirred the brew, then held it out for Sara's inspection. "The latest from the Chez Theodora espresso bar: cardamom cockroach supreme."

Sara peered into the mug. "Oh, yuk! Where did they come from?"

"As of a moment ago, the can of milk. But I believe I brought them aboard in the cardboard boxes that held our stores."

"So how do we get rid of them?"

Matt dumped his new blend in the sink. "We can try boric acid, it's pretty harmless stuff. But if we can't find any or things get out of hand I guess we can gas the suckers."

"Let's do it soon," Sara said. "I heard that if you see one there's a hundred in hiding."

Theodora, back from her restless night with Porky, grumbled, "More like two hundred by my count." She had had a fitful time plagued by creepy dreams of roaches prancing on her ankles. So real was the sensation, she'd awakened several times to swat them away.

After Breakfast, Matt and Sara decided to row ashore for boric acid or roach spray. Once on deck, Matt noticed the dinghy tied forward, snug against *TR's* hull. "Did you move the dinghy?" he asked.

Sara shook her head. "Last I saw, it was trailing behind where we left it. You think someone used it?"

Matt surveyed the anchorage, shading his eyes with one hand. A few charter boats were anchored astern and they all had dinghies. He shrugged. "Weird. If someone did use it, at least they returned it."

After that, Theodora was careful about returning Porky's painter to the sternrail.

Chapter 16

Armed with an outdated can of Baygon Ant & Roach spray—the boric acid would have to wait for more sophisticated shopping opportunities—Matt took a defensive position against the cockroaches. In the evenings, whenever he or Sara spotted one of the creatures peeping out from some gap in the joinery, he'd whip the spray-can into action. Unfortunately, a weak spurt was all the can would produce, and a startled roach would scurry away unscathed. Matt was sure the bugs snickered at his efforts.

Theodora bemoaned Matt's actions and whined to Thelma, "Pathetic, just pathetic. What good are a few dead roaches with thousands in reserve. It's like attacking the advance guard of Alexander's army. We'll never be rid of the damn things."

Thelma listened with feigned interest, secretly delighted at the queen's plight. Yes, they had roaches, but not quite an infestation. The last four nights she'd seen the queen sleeping aboard Porky, and even witnessed Porky fondling Theodora's ankles while she slept. She didn't think it her place to reprimand the boy for taking liberties. It seemed an odd, yet harmless, fetish and added realism to the queen's nightmares of roach attacks. "It's a problem indeed, Missy. The situation will surely get worse before it gets better. The buggers are clever, only a few ever venture into the open and they propagate faster than urchins in a tide pool. Our Matt won't have a clue until we're overrun." She loved to bait the queen and it did her heart good to see the witch squirm.

Theodora would be damned if she'd wait for Matt to learn of the growing number of roaches in her hull. That night, as they lay sheltered from another northerly blow, she went to work in earnest on the stainless steel hoseclamp that attached the sink drain to a thru-hull fitting below the water line. It took all her compromised power to budge the adjusting nut. "Flush you bastards out." she huffed after a small tweak of the nut. A thin stream of saltwater began to dribble from the hose. Theodora stood back, dusted off her hands. "Sink or swim, fishbait."

Instantly aware of the leak, Thelma went to investigate. "What are you up to, Missy?"

"Like you said, until the captain sees all the roaches, we're stuck with 'em. As soon as I flood our bilge, he'll know what he's dealing with."

Thelma pushed the queen aside and reached for the hoseclamp. "Lord, Missy, that leak is below our waterline. We could sink. We're nowhere near a repair facility if anything should go wrong." She gave the nut a mighty wrench but it was stuck fast. Water continued to flow into their bilge. "Lend a hand here. I don't like the feel of this."

Jarred by the word 'sink', Theodora obeyed without question. Unfortunately, their combined efforts couldn't retighten the nut. If anything, their messing with the clamp increased the flow of water.

Thelma stood back, hands on hips. "You've sailed the wrong course this time, Missy."

Theodora stuck a manicured finger in Thelma's face. "You want to live with roaches, fine. Not me! There's plenty of shallow water around here and the captain can always beach us. Besides, he pumps our bilge every day."

She pushed the queen's hand away. "We'll have to trust him to stop the leak then, won't we? Let's just hope he doesn't go to sea."

At dawn, Matt went on deck to check the anchor, the state of the wind and to relieve himself. The last being the most important, not just because his bladder demanded release, but the act itself. For Matt, peeing over the side was such poignant expression of freedom that it had become a necessary ritual to start the day. Positioned at the leeward shrouds, one arm locked around the aftermost, he released his water to the sea, completing another cycle of nature.

The wind had lost its weight, and what now blew from the northwest in a steady tease was his fair-wind sail to the east. He leaned over the forward hatch. "Wakey, wakey. All hands on deck and prepare to make sail."

Sara peeked out from under the sheet and squinted up at him. "Really? Now?"

"Yup. It's our easy ride to the Virgin Islands." In his best Hornblower voice he added, "There's not a moment to lose!"

He trotted to the stern, hauled *Porky* aboard and popped his rubber corks. As the dinghy sagged to a rag, he and Sara stashed everything safely in its rightful place below. Half an hour later, they sailed from the protection of Cherokee Sound at the south end of the Abacos. He plotted a course out the New Providence Channel to the Atlantic. Should the wind fail them, Matt figured he had several options for another layover in the outer Bahamian islands or the Turks and Caicos before reaching Puerto Rico and the Virgin Islands beyond.

The two spirits stood at the bow as they sailed into the bottomless Atlantic. Thelma couldn't help herself, she had to rub it in. "Where's your shallow water now, eh, luv? And in case you hadn't noticed, our Matt was a wee bit hasty and missed our bilge this morning."

The queen lowered her head and closed her eyes. *Mother of God, I'll never hear the end of this. It might be worth sinking just to shut the old biddy up.* "Yeah," she said, "I noticed, but we're only half full and the roaches are on the run."

Thelma sniffed. "Roaches will be the least of our worries if things get out of hand."

Exasperated, the queen turned on Thelma. "Why all the drama? It's a small leak for chrissake! Our bilge pump can handle it."

"Yes," Thelma sighed, "the bilge pump." What's the use, she thought. Only those of us with years of experience in a saltwater world would understand. Theodora was too new, and too naive to appreciate how a small problem could fester into a catastrophe at sea.

Reaching into the south-southeast, the fresh breeze kept the main and genoa under a firm press, and earthy smells followed them offshore. Whitecaps frosted the chop, and high tendrils of cirrus clouds stole the warmth from the sun.

The easterly Atlantic swell gave *TR* an awkward roll and Sara began to yawn. She stretched out on the cockpit seat, pulled the collar of her green sweater up to her ears, and shut her eyes.

"Feel okay?" Matt asked.

"Just tired, but I feel like I'm on a carnival ride."

"Yeah, after three weeks of flat water I'm even feeling a little weird from this corkscrew motion. As soon as I get Fred hooked up we can relax and let him steer."

"Good. I'm in no mood to watch that compass-card swing."

By the time Matt convinced Fred to keep the proper course and rigged a preventer on the boom in case he strayed, Great Abaco was a thin, gray smudge on the horizon. Sara began to moan; soft whimpers at first, but as the morning wore on they strengthened to hollow gut-wrenchers that nearly had Matt in tears of pity.

Not good. This is a death roll for our relationship. If it keeps up I'll be without a mate for sure. He tried to picture himself sailing alone then changed the subject. The possibility was too painful to confront.

It wasn't until noon, and they were thirty miles into the Atlantic Ocean, that Matt finally had the desire to eat. He ventured below for the first time since leaving the anchorage. Stepping beyond the last rung on the companionway ladder, his foot touched water.

Chapter 17

Matt froze on the ladder. His heart skipped a beat, and his mind hit hyperdrive. It zipped past What the hell? Oh, shit! Holy fuck! 'Get a grip!' and stopped on, "Uh oh."

Sara lifted her pale face. "Uh oh, what?"

He worked to keep his voice calm. "I'm standing in water." His hand went to the switch for the electric bilge pump–nothing. No soft whir. No discharge on the amp gauge. 'Oh, shit!' came round again.

Sara shot upright. "Water? You mean we're sinking?"

"Not yet, but there's definitely a leak. He waved a hand at the helm. "Disconnect Fred and heave-to while I have a look."

He turned the battery switch from ENGINE to CABIN. The amp gauge jumped and he felt the light vibration of the pump.

TR rolled sharply to port. A ponderous mass of water sloshed in the bilge. The teak floorboards of the cabin sole floated free. Matt shoved the heavy planks to one side and stepped into the bilge. He sank to his knees.

Cans of beer bobbed around the cabin, nudging his legs like a school of hungry fish. There were three thru-hull fittings below the waterline. It made sense to start with those. He'd serviced them all six weeks ago and knew them intimately. He groped for the nearest one, the engine intake. The handle swung shut with ease.

Another lurch to port. A surge of water. The sizzle of liberated electricity. The smell of ozone.

Sara screamed. "Matt! There's smoke coming from the engine hatch."

Matt yanked open the door to the engine room. Acrid smoke billowed out. "Shit, fried the starter. No wonder the battery's dead," he muttered, then yelled to Sara, "It's okay. No fire."

The bilge pump still hummed. He waded forward to the head, closed that fitting. He fumbled with the locker under the galley sink, tossed aside pots and pans and closed the remaining thru-hull. A quick survey of the sloshing water assured him that at least it wasn't rising fast.

He climbed to the cockpit. *TR* rode quietly, locked in the wind. Sara had just winched in the mainsail and looked exhausted from the effort. Her skin, tinged with green, stretched tight on her face. He answered her panicked expression with a firm grip on her shoulder. "I think it's under control."

He glanced over the side, saw a solid stream of frothy water gushing from the bilge pump exhaust then turned back to Sara. "We'll know in a couple of minutes if we're on top of it." He dug a couple of plastic buckets out of a cockpit locker. "They say there's no better pump then a scared man with a bucket. Let's bail this puppy out."

Stripped to the waist, Matt stood with his feet braced on either side of the bilge. He scooped up buckets of water, swung them to the cockpit and Sara chucked the contents to Poseidon.

As the water level dropped, his concentration on the task wavered. That's when he noticed the activity. It seemed peripheral at first, a fleeting sense of motion. He focused on one corner of the settee. Three roaches scurried across the cushion. He shifted his gaze. Half a dozen milled about on the table. A small herd charged around the galley sink. So much for the Baygon, he thought. Sara would freak. He decided to keep the prolific wildlife to himself, hoping it would disappear once the bilge was dry.

Theodora, who watched the fiasco from the forward hatch, clapped her hands with joy. She called to Thelma who was pacing the deck. "It worked! He saw the roaches."

Thelma slapped the palm of her hand to her forehead. *What can that silly nit be thinking? She floods our bilge on the high seas, our engine battery is dead, the starter motor kaput and still she thinks about roaches.* "So what do you expect our captain to do? Get on the VHF and call an exterminator?"

"We all have our priorities," the queen said. "Mine happens to be the bugs. There's nothing wrong with our sails and Matt can handle us without an engine."

Thelma ceased her pacing and leaned one shoulder against the mast. "You're right, he doesn't need the iron genny, but he's got a lot to learn and that motor is handy in a pinch."

Theodora spread her arms and looked around the endless blue horizon. "So what's to worry. No land, good weather...isn't that a sailor's dream?"

The spirits were interrupted by Sara, who screeched and danced a wild jig in the cockpit. She tossed her bucket aside, ripped at the zipper on her jeans and wiggled frantically from the pants. She hadn't worn any underwear. She swatted madly at the roach patrol climbing her leg, advancing on the bikini line. "Ugh! you bastards...off."

Oh, boy, just what she needed. He lifted the full bucket in his hands and doused her legs and butt. Sara howled from the shock and burst into tears.

Matt fetched a towel from the head and handed it up to her.

She wrapped it around her waist, plopped down on a wet cushion and wept.

Thelma shook a finger at the queen who displayed a sneering grin. "Not a word, Missy. You'd have acted like a hot tuna in a bathtub if you'd had roaches in your nickers."

Matt tried humor. "I forgot to tell you, I think we have a roach problem."

Sara glared. Matt kept bailing.

Finally, the pump made dry sucking sounds. The last of the water dribbled into the sea. It only took Matt a few minutes to find the leak in the galley, which, when he opened the valve, had grown to a healthy jet. He tightened the hose-clamp. *How the hell did that come loose?* He checked the other thru-hull fittings, added a second clamp to each for good measure, then joined Sara in the cockpit.

She sat, clutching her knees, staring out to sea.

"I found the problem," he said. "A leak under the sink. All fixed now."

No response. Not a blink.

"Bummer about the roaches. I'll get something potent as soon as we hit port." Matt waited.

She spoke in a whisper. "I want off."

"We don't have any Off. Only the Baygon."

She exploded. "No, God damn it! I want off this fucking boat!"

"Shit, Sara, it was only a few little bugs and some water in the bilge. Why so testy?"

She turned and faced him. "No, Matt, it wasn't a few bugs and water in the bilge. They were the icing on the cake of misery. I'm sick, I'm bored, I miss my friends, this is third-class living and I've had enough."

"But..."

She put a finger to his lips. "I don't think you really care about me in the big picture. You want a bed-warmer and a yes-man and I can't do that."

He pulled her hand down. "That's not true, Sara. I do care about you, but nothing I'm doing interests you. What am I supposed to do?"

She flashed a wry smile. "I know we're only forty miles from Nassau. Take me there and I'll fly home."

Matt knew that voice. She'd made up her mind. He felt a twang in his chest as if a halyard had parted. "Look," he said, "how about we blow off this jump to the Virgins and we'll cruise the whole island chain east. There'll be plenty of calm water." He didn't add 'and things to see'. She hadn't changed on that front.

She gave a slow shake of her head as if it required extreme effort. "It'll just be more of the same. Always your call. Trips ashore, visits to other boats. The only reason I like to visit other yachts is for the drinks. It helps pass the time."

Jesus, how did I miss that?

"Surely you knew this would come. I'm not what you expected...I'm sorry...but there it is."

"Shit, Babe. I didn't realize it was that bad. Listen, why don't I run you all the way back to Lauderdale? It'll give us a little more time."

Sara barked a laugh. "For what? Me to lose more weight? Hell, Matt, if I thought I could swim to Nassau I'd be in the water now. That's how bad I'm feeling. Get it?"

He locked eyes with her for a moment then he reached out and squeezed her knee. "Got it."

Five minutes later they were on course for Nassau, clipping along at six knots with an uncomfortable pitch caused by the following sea.

Matt removed the saltwater drenched starter from the engine and gave it a fresh-water rinse before it had a chance to corrode. The plastic cap on the solenoid had melted, but with the help of Five-Minute Epoxy he was able to begin a repair. It would take a couple days to make things right. But the lack of an engine would force him to be a sailing purist.

That evening, the wind died with the sun. By dark, the ocean surface had glassed over –the bane of the sailing purist. The only ripples were from *TR's* hull, lurching in the residual swell. Her mainsail slatted with violent snaps as she rocked like a cradle gone wild. Below, a symphony of loosely stored items played a clattering ode to the sea, while above, the only sound was an occasional dry retch from Sara interspersed with, "Please God, only thirty more miles."

Matt saw it as the *coup de gräce* for any chance of reconciliation. The sea would turn to fresh water before Sara stepped foot on a boat again. He cursed the day's events, blamed himself for his part. If only they'd stayed another few days at anchor. If only he'd picked a flat day for a short hop to Spanish Wells. If only, if only....

He flipped on the masthead light as a means to warn any possible shipping traffic. The tired cabin battery only produced a feeble glow, so instead he rigged a kerosene lamp from the boom. It shone with a soft yellow light and twirled like a dance partner in *TR's* arms.

At midnight, Matt's eyelids felt like they were wearing dive weights. "Hey. Sara, you awake?"

"Unfortunately, yes," she grumbled.

"Would you keep an eye out? I gotta get some shuteye." She didn't move from her prone position on the bench. "Uh huh."

Matt vaguely recalled laying his head on the pillow when he was suddenly shaken awake. Sara hovered over him, panicked eyes, breath in gasps. "Come, quick!"

They scrambled to the cockpit. The deep throb of a huge engine vibrated the night like a death chant.

Astern, Matt saw red and green running lights and between them two white directional lights, one directly above the other– collision course. "What's the matter with that guy! Can't he ... Jesus! Our lamp's out." He dove below, grabbed a powerful six-volt flashlight. Back in the cockpit he aimed the beam at the lights. The bow of a giant vessel loomed above. He saw the bow wave, purled over in a foam crest. He jiggled the light back and forth.

BAUUUUUUUUUU. The blast from the ship's air-horn hit them like a gust of cold wind. Matt's yell almost smothered Sara's scream. He locked her in his arms, sure they'd be plowed under.

The white lights split. The red light vanished. A steep frothy wave rocked *TR* on her beam ends.

They were tossed across the cockpit and Matt's hip slammed into a winch. A black wall churned by, a yard from *TR's* stern. The deck shook. Diesel smoke left them hacking.

Seconds later, the night dissolved in the piercing cone of an arclight. Matt shielded his eyes, but he was blinded. He heard the ship engine throttled back, the whir of heavy machinery. Then another engine—a small diesel.

A stout, heavily bumpered, thirty-foot skiff chugged into the circle of light; there were three figures on board. The man at the helm conned the vessel along side *TR* with an expert hand. A robust woman in a yellow slicker leaned over the side. "You folks okay?" she hailed.

Matt stepped to the deck so he was only a few feet away. His legs still shook and his hip throbbed. "Lost a few years is all."

"Why ain't you runnin' lights? Bout gave my husband a coronary."

"System failures," Matt said. "Had a kerosene lamp. Must have gone out. My fault. Sorry."

"Bet you got some shorts to wash."

"Tell me about it. Thanks for stopping. Name's Matt."

"Marge Winkler, off the Colossus out of Houston. Ocean goin' tug. On our way to Miami."

"Mr. Winkler gets the medal for sharp eyes," Matt said.

Marge conferred with the guy behind her, then turned back. "Anything you need to get things runnin'?"

Matt thought a minute, but knew a jump-start was out of the question. He was about to decline the offer when Sara crowded beside him. "How about a lift?" she yelled.

Chapter 18

There was a shocked pause, only the burble of engines. "You serious?" Marge asked.

Sara nodded. "I'm seasick as hell and can't wait to get off this tub."

Matt looked at Sara. She wouldn't meet his eye—the end. He turned back to Marge. "Yeah," he added, "she is."

Another short conference, this one on a hand-held radio, with the skipper. Matt heard a staccato voice on the radio say, "Okay by me."

Marge looked up. "Get yer gear, honey. We got a schedule to keep."

Thelma had seen people jump ship before, but never at sea. She watched Sara lunge through the boat, cramming clothes, personal odds and ends into a duffel. Matt followed her around in silence, handing her things she'd missed, a brush, a pair of sneakers, a photo of her parents. When the duffel was full, she glanced around. "If I missed anything, give it to someone needy." She knelt on the bag, forced the zipper shut, then stood and faced Matt. "Sorry it turned out this way."

Matt reached out and pulled her to his chest. "Me, too." She returned the squeeze, but there were no kisses.

On deck, Matt tossed the full duffel across two feet of open water to the skiff. He took Sara's hand and passed her to Marge Winkler. Marge yanked her aboard and the boat rumbled off. Sara turned and waved. Matt lifted one hand and let it drop. He watched until the lights of the Colossus vanished in the night.

A soft rain began to fall. Thelma sat on the cabin top, feet firmly planted on the deck, elbows on knees, chin on fists, pushing her face into a pout. She felt her seventy-plus years in every joint. At the point of near collision, she'd been sure she'd caught her last breeze. She expected to feel her timbers crunch, see the splinters fly, sense the slow tumble to a thousand fathom grave.

And the precious queen! Why she'd been oblivious to the tug's approach, so wrapped up she was in her early celebration of Sara's imminent departure. It wasn't until Thelma had dragged her from her reverie, to help alert a barely conscious Sara that the queen realized they were in danger. Between the two of them, they were able to swing the clapper on the ship's bell with enough force to produce a clang that made Sara look up. At the instant destruction loomed, Theodora had squealed and fled up the mast. Thelma tilted her weary head back, rollers askew, and peered upward. *Yup, still there, still clutching the spruce with her eyes shut. I doubt the frightened dear even knows Sara's gone. It'll probably be daylight before she works up the nerve to come down.*

Matt relit the kerosene lamp then stepped into the cockpit. His gaze wandered from the wheel, to the compass, to the sheet winches and finally rested on the steering vane he'd named Fred. "I guess it's just you and me Freddy boy." As an afterthought he patted the fir planking on *TR's* bridge deck. "And you, too, Old Girl."

Sara's abrupt departure had left him hovering in a state of denial. He worked to stay there, knowing that eventually he would take the fall and have to confront the inevitable disappointment. Like a wind tattered sail, his emotions would require a patch and a few stitches before he could catch another fresh breeze.

Seven days later Matt stood on the plunging foredeck, leaning against the mast for support. He scanned the southern horizon with his Steiner binoculars. "Where the hell is it?" he muttered. According to his calculations he should have seen the high volcanic island of St. Thomas at sunrise. It was now almost noon.

After Sara jumped ship, he'd made the decision to learn celestial navigation, not using the GPS for this passage. The challenge was to go the traditional route with sextant, stopwatch and the navy's H.O.249 sight reduction tables. For the last week, he'd been teaching himself the rudiments of the art from a thin text written by a man named Kittredge who offered a basic cookbook approach that left little room for error. Handling the sextant had been easy, but the math was deceptively simple and it tended to trip him up. Maybe he'd been too hasty. If he'd screwed up too much, he might be sailing into reef-strewn waters. He was sorely tempted to turn on the magic box and let the GPS ease his mind, but no, that would be cheating. Puzzled, Matt went below to check the figures on his last two sun shots.

The weeklong open passage from the Bahamas had left him little time to dwell on his now solo adventure. Within hours of becoming a singlehanded sailor, a moderate tradewind had filled in from the northeast. The last thing Matt had wanted to do was sit at anchor somewhere and think about his loss. The favorable wind and knowing he had willing crew in Fred helped him choose the six hundred miles of open Atlantic over the slow island-hop to St. Thomas.

Thelma was delighted with his decision. For her, there was nothing quite the equal to romping over the endless ocean swells. She felt charged with a vitality that she hadn't felt since the colonel had sailed her over from England. She didn't even mind the thin, salted slices of fish drying on her deck—the remains of a fifty-pound tuna Matt had caught the second day out.

She grudgingly admitted to the queen that it seemed they were better off without Sara.

"Seems? Hell!" Theodora said. "It's a fact. He has time for *us* now. No way we'd have gotten new oil on our bowsprit or baggywrinkles on our shrouds if he'd been dealing with the moods of the crew."

"Mind you," said Thelma, "that will all come to an end as soon as we hit port. I've seen it before after days at sea. Frolicking ashore has something to do with feeding a sailor's soul."

"Well I'd rather be in port than out here with a few miserable fish," the queen said. "Our roach population is growing like fungus, the jerked tuna on deck reeks and there's no one around to appreciate the work Matt has done to enhance my beauty."

Thelma ignored the queen after that. She'd been built for the sea, not for being seen.

Matt climbed back to the cockpit, satisfied that he'd made no mistakes. His gaze went back to the horizon. Nothing. But when he sat back and looked at the sky he saw it—a dark outline that stretched across his entire view. He hadn't figured on visibility being under ten miles. Soon, the green humps of St. Thomas emerged from the ocean haze, looking like some long extinct reptile basking in the midday sun. Matt's spirits soared. He held up a clenched fist and yelled, "Right on!"

Approaching from the north, he steered a course for the east end of the island where his spiral-bound cruising guide told him he'd find a good anchorage and supplies at Red Hook Bay. *TR* was still without a working engine, but he'd finished repairing the starter motor. All he needed now was to have the batteries charged. He realized now that he should have had an alternative source of electric power from the beginning, either solar power or a small generator. He would remedy that.

The north shore was smothered with coconut palms, creepers and vines, and the Atlantic swells creamed the beach. Only a few roofs poked through the vegetation. As he rounded the island he entered the rain shadow, where a brown arid landscape seemed cluttered with industrial growth.

Fluky winds gave Matt a workout keeping the main and jib filled, tacking every few minutes—anything to maintain steerage.

Gotta get the motor running, he thought. It's the only insurance I have.

The heavy boat traffic near Red Hook upped his stress level beyond anything he'd felt at sea. The Bahamas had been a scene of tranquility compared to this. He sailed amid dozens of charter boats, jet-skis and two ferries. The air was tinged with engine exhaust and the racket competed with motorized civilization ashore.

Red Hook was crammed with anchored craft. Matt didn't dare sail into that mess. He dropped anchor at the wide entrance of the deep cut and set the plow firmly with the last of *TR's* momentum. He exhaled a deep sigh of relief when she turned her bow to the wind.

As he furled the sails, a sixty-foot ferry rumbled by only fifty yards away. The big props churned the water to a pale blue. It set up a wake that rolled *TR* through ninety degrees, a violent swing far worse than being at sea. In the turbulent water behind the ferry, a small dark head popped up. Matt heard a scream.

Chapter 19

Matt didn't hesitate. He leapt from the foredeck, pierced the water in a shallow dive, and surfaced in a strong crawl. He kept his eye on the bobbing head, afraid he'd lose sight of the child.

At twenty yards, Matt saw two pointy ears and heard another scream. This one sounded more like a distressed meow. He slowed his pace. *A damn cat.* There was panic in the animal's one good eye; the other was opaque white. Matt stopped at ten feet, wary of the claws on a freaked out feline. He glanced at the receding ferry but there were no concerned faces at the stern.

The cat appeared to be swimming okay, so he coaxed it along. "C'mon tiger, come with me." He set off in a slow sidestroke back to the boat. The cat followed. "Hang in there, buddy, just a few more feet." Matt pulled himself up and over TR's bulwarks, grabbed up a coiled sheet line and hung it over the side. The cat swam straight for the makeshift ladder. He sank his claws into the bundle of rope and climbed aboard.

Even soaking wet it was a big cat: male, gray with black stripes and a quarter-inch nick out of its right ear. Matt guessed he weighed in at a good fifteen pounds. The cat shook himself off and stalked up and down the deck, twisting his massive head back and forth, probably to accommodate the good eye.

Matt ducked below, changed his sodden shorts for dry ones, and snagged a chunk of dry tuna before returning topside. He squatted and held out his hand. "Feeding time, big guy. Come 'n get it."

The cat trotted up and sniffed the offering. He eased it from Matt's fingers with a gentle mouth and sat at his feet. Matt stroked the animal's back while it scarfed the snack. "How did you end up in the drink? The old lady kick ya' out?"

The cat purred like an old outboard with a carburetor problem. Matt felt the vibration in the deck.

"Sounds like you could use a tune-up. Sit tight. I'll run you ashore in a minute."

Theodora and Thelma watched the scene from the cabin roof. The queen wiped imaginary sweat from her brow. "Whew, for a second, I thought Matt would keep him. Did you see the claws on that monster? Even when he looks at our sails, I get shivers."

"The colonel kept a cat aboard for a while," Thelma said. "Black as tar, it was. Shredded the cushion on the port settee as regular as the spring tide, but the old man loved the bloody thing. Make great companions, cats do."

"We just got rid of Sara," the queen said. "We need another companion like we need another roach."

"I'm not so sure our captain feels the same," Thelma said.

They watched Matt inflate Porky. When the tubby spirit gained substance, he was clearly upset, knees together, hands clasped, face twisted in distress.

"What's the matter, lad?" Thelma asked.

Porky jabbed a shaky finger at the feline sniffing his pontoons. "Th...the cat, Thelma. Sharp claws."

Thelma rested a hand on his shoulder. "Not to worry, dear. The Captain knows."

Flipping Porky over the side, Matt tied him securely against TR's hull. He loaded the dead engine battery into Porky's bow, then used more tuna to lure the cat within grasp. When Matt lifted the fifteen-pound fur-ball over the side, the animal went rigid, legs out, claws extended.

Porky freaked. His shoulders hunched. He threw one arm across his eyes. "I can't watch," he cried. "I'll be torn to pieces."

Matt sat at Porky's stern, lowered the cat to his lap and spoke in a soothing tone. "Easy, boy. We're going for a short ride." He stroked the big head and the paws collapsed, claws withdrew. "Jeeze, you're a hefty sucker. Bet you're the town bully." He lowered him to the rubber floor.

Porky held his breath and peeked from behind his arm. "Nice, kitty," he cooed. "Nice kitty."

When Matt picked up the oars, the cat moved to the bow, raised his head and appeared to give Porky the once-over with his clear eye. Then he lifted one paw, spread a sinister fan of needle-sharp claws and slowly licked the pad of his foot.

Porky broke out in a cold sweat, imagination run amuck. He could just feel the claws rake his inflated pontoons, hear the hiss of escaping air. He knew the cat couldn't see him, but had the uncanny feeling that the animal was aware of his presence.

As if in response to that very thought, it seemed to Porky the cat looked him in the eye and winked.

Matt rowed through the maze of anchored craft, negotiating a web of anchor lines and tethered dinghies. At the head of the bay, a dozen tenders were clustered around a small wooden dock. He couldn't help but notice they all had steel cable painters with locks. He nudged Porky into the pack, tied him up, then spoke to the cat. "End of the line, bud."

Porky cringed when the cat leaped to the dock but he didn't feel the slightest prick from its claws. Matt wrestled the battery from the soft floor of the dinghy. Not used to solid footing, he stumbled down the jetty with the fifty-pound load. The cat followed him ashore.

At a small boatyard nearby, a young black man took the battery and told him it would be ready in the morning. He glanced at the cat whose ragged purr demanded comment. "You leavin' him for a tune-up?"

Matt laughed. "No, but I'd like to find out who he belongs to."

The guy shook his head. "Can't help."

"Any place nearby I can check e-mail?"

The guy gestured with his chin. "Bar just down the road."

Matt thanked him and headed out. He was anxious to know how Sara had fared on her trip home. It didn't take long.

Matt, The folks on Colossus couldn't have been nicer. I was back with my parents the next day. I'm really, really, really glad to be back. Sorry it didn't work out. I'm sure you'll get by just fine. Keep in touch. Sara

He shot her an equally short reply, thinking he was really, really, really glad she was gone.

Outside, the cat waited in the shade. "Well, big guy, I guess it could have been worse. We could have been married."

Matt walked to the St. Johns ferry terminal, the cat at his heels. Traffic, vintage vehicles from the sixties and seventies, zoomed by on the narrow blacktop. Nobody at the terminal knew the cat, but he was told there were plenty of strays around.

At a small market, Matt loaded up on fresh fruit, a bag of ice and a two-dollar quart of Cruzan rum. He also found an impressive display of roach killers. The old woman at the checkout told him boric acid was their best seller.

So I'm not the only one with roach problems. He gladly paid six dollars for a box of the white powder then headed back to the dinghy. The cat trotted in his shadow.

Matt stowed his purchases aboard *Porky* and stooped to pet his friend. "You're on your own now, buddy. When I come in tomorrow, I'll bring some of that tuna in case I see you." The cat followed him into the dinghy. Mat scooped him up and set him back on the dock. "No you don't. I have enough trouble taking care of myself."

As Matt rowed back to *TR*, he caught glimpses of the cat, a furtive movement along the shore, paralleling his course.

No, I don't need a cat. Think of the litter box and all the food that big old cat would eat–not to mention quarantine problems in foreign countries. No. Definitely not.

Matt looked forward to a quiet evening at anchor–no sail changes, no navigation problems, no half-hour horizon checks, just sleep. By the time he'd finished his fourth rum punch and second bowl of popcorn drenched in garlic butter, it was dark.

He spread the boric acid judiciously throughout the bilge and made his final entries in the logbook. He hung the kerosene lamp as an anchor light and lounged in the cockpit. Lights shone in most of the boats around him. Voices, music and the smell of grilled steaks carried across the water. The alcohol had given him a relaxed buzz and he mused about the success of his first open passage. He had doubted his ability to handle *TR* on his own after Sara left, but soon realized that with her touchy stomach she wouldn't have been much help anyway. He felt a strong sense of pride that he had made the passage on his own, but missed having someone to share it with. He imagined what Sara would be doing in Florida–probably she'd be back at the antique shop. He pictured her with her friends, making light of her great misadventure.

Like an unexpected shift in the wind, the chill breeze of loneliness wafted in and engulfed Matt's heart. He took a deep breath and a last swig of rum, then went to bed.

These musings did not escape Thelma, who sensed her captain's morose feelings. She'd known her original owner and the colonel to both have bouts of loneliness, which she took to be common among singlehanders. Her only worry was whether this would be a passing cloud or a major depression that would remain stationary for days or weeks. She'd heard tales of lonely sailors getting stuck in tropical watering holes for years where cheap rum worked like a permanent mooring.

She knew the queen would be no help. A tot of rum and a good laugh meant more to her than going to sea. And now that Matt had the roaches on the run, Theodora would soon be comfortable again. When they'd sailed in that afternoon, the trollop had her hand mirror out before the anchor was down. She had strutted the deck over flattering comments shouted by crews from passing yachts. The one that had really swelled her head was, "She oughtta be on the cover of Wooden Boat." Thelma had even enjoyed that one. Matt had several issues of the magazine on the bookshelf next to his bunk. For now, Thelma could do little more than knock over the rum bottle Matt had left in the cockpit. She watched the dregs of the 'Pirate's Passion' run down the cockpit drain.

Chapter 20

Thelma and the queen watched the cat scramble aboard about midnight. Thelma had to admire its tenacity. They were anchored a good hundred yards from shore and the beast would be a bite-size morsel for any hungry night-feeder.

"Terrific," Theodora said with enough disgust to make the cat hiss. She cocked her head and peered at him. He stared back. She moved behind Thelma. "What do you make of that?"

Thelma grunted. "I'd say you'd better watch your mouth. It's bad luck to provoke a ship's cat. It's known they have a sense of the spirit world."

"His dead eye gives me the creeps," the queen said. "I have a bad feeling about him. I see hairballs and the delicate scent of cat piss in our future."

Thelma wanted to say, "It might balance out the nauseous cologne you wear," but she also knew it was bad luck to provoke the queen.

The cat stretched out on a cockpit cushion and began grooming his coat, a long, hypnotic process.

Both spirits kept a wary eye on his claws.

He was still there when a silent figure rowed alongside and began picking at the knot on Porky's painter.

Thelma, shocked at the brazen act, fretted over what to do. Finally, she grabbed the queen's wrist and made for the ship's bell, the only alarm that came to mind.

But before they were even close, the cat sprang from the cockpit with a blood-freezing cry and slashed the man's arm.

The maniacal screech jolted Matt from a rum-laced sleep. He heard the clatter of oars and a hissed "Ah, *merde*!." He vaulted naked through the forward hatch and onto the deck to investigate. A man in a small dinghy rowed rapidly from the stern of *TR* into the dark. The splash and flash of the oars lingered when all else had disappeared. Then he heard the purr. Matt whirled and looked down. He broke out laughing. "Well, if it isn't old Tune-up." The cat rubbed against his leg. Its fur was damp.

Matt scanned the deck. "What's going on here?" He noticed the coil of line was still hanging over the side where he'd left it. "Swam out and invited yourself aboard, did ya?"

He walked to the stern to check on the dinghy. It was still there, but the knot holding its painter to *TR's* lifeline was half untied. He refastened it and thought about the cables and locks he'd seen on the other dinghies ashore. He mused over the sequence of events.

The screech must have been the cat. His fur was only damp, so he must have been here a while. Looks like someone tried to make off with my dinghy. On the bulwarks, beneath where the dinghy was tied, there were two drops of what could only be fresh blood. He knelt and examined each of the cat's front feet. Small shreds of what appeared to be skin clung to the claws of the left paw.

Matt appraised the cat with a new respect. *Maybe he wouldn't eat too much and quarantine procedures might not be as strict as they used to be.* He scratched the cat behind the ears, triggering its coarse, sputtering purr. "Well Tune-up, looks like you might have a job. Seems I need someone around to discourage thieves and repel boarders." Matt chuckled and boxed him lightly on the chin.

"I reckon we've got a new first mate," Thelma said. "It's obvious he's got our welfare and that of young Porky at heart. I think he'll be a great friend to Matt."

Theodora wrinkled her nose in distaste, picked a strand of cat hair off her white gown and held it out to Thelma. "This is just the beginning. Wait 'til he starts sharpening those claws. He'll make toothpicks of our mast."

She batted the queen's hand away. "I wish for once you could see beyond your own vanity, Missy. Our Matt has a liking for rum and a hollow spot in his heart to fill. Best it be Tune-up here that fills it. Your fancy paint job and windowpane varnish will go the way of a work scow if he takes a fancy to the bottle."

Theodora stepped up to Thelma, fists hard on her hips, crimson lips in a thin line. "Who are you? The temperance league? It won't hurt the captain to have a few drinks. Do him good to loosen up and party. We've just had a week of your bounding main and signed on a diesel-powered cat for crew. Lighten up, you old bat."

Thelma cinched up her belt. "Old bat, indeed," she huffed. In good conscience, she couldn't argue with any of the points the queen made regarding Matt. *Maybe I'm asking a bit too much. We've only been in port twelve hours, and I suppose the captain's entitled to a fling.*

Matt fed the cat a chunk of dried tuna and returned to bed. In the morning, after setting a kettle to boil, he began as usual to sluice the decks with saltwater, killing any rot spores carried in the fresh water of the morning dew. He could feel last night's alcohol—stiff muscles, blood turned to sludge and a tongue that rivaled the cat's pelt.

Beside the aft scupper on the port side sat a tidy pile of cat poop. One shot with a full bucket carried it through the scupper and over the side. *Not bad.* He spoke to Tune-up who still snoozed in the cockpit. "Got your own little poop deck here, huh? I have to say your credentials are impeccable: guard cat, requires no litterbox, eats what's at hand. Guess that makes you a keeper."

Tune-up rolled to his back, stretched full-length then snapped to his feet. The uneven rumble of his purr seemed an acknowledgement of his new appointment.

While Matt sipped his morning coffee, the first ferry churned by, rocking *TR* to such an extreme that Matt's mug sloshed over. The empty rum bottle clattered onto the cockpit floor. For a brief instant, a part of Matt's brain mourned the loss of the rum. He picked up the bottle. "Enough rolling around. We're outta here."

He rowed ashore, retrieved his battery then stopped at the market for a sack of cat food. Ahead of him in the checkout was a tall, bronze, skinny guy in a very brief yellow swimsuit, who spoke with a French accent to the cashier. There was a fresh bandage wrapped around his right forearm and he was buying hydrogen peroxide. Matt asked him what happened. The guy picked up his bag of groceries as if he hadn't heard the question, but just as he walked off he said, "*Le chat* from hell."

Outside the market was a public bulletin board. Matt still wanted a back-up energy source. He scanned the ads for a generator or solar panel, all the while keeping an eye on the guy in the yellow trunks.

One of the yachts at anchor in Red Hook had a single forty-five watt solar panel with regulator for two hundred bucks. Matt made note of the vessel's name and returned to his dinghy.

From the jetty he watched Yellow Trunks row up to a lackluster aluminum sloop with a tattered, sun-bleached French flag hung on the backstay. Two brown mutts lounged on the foredeck. Got your number, he thought, then rowed out. As he passed the stern of the French boat he read the name *Cher,* and filed it away in his memory.

Not far from *TR* was a fifty-foot fiberglass ketch with the name corresponding to the ad. Matt rowed alongside.

An hour later, Tune-up welcomed him back aboard. Matt showed him his almost new Arco solar panel. "Guaranteed to crank out three amps per hour in good sun. Should be plenty. What do you think?"

Tune-up croaked a feeble meow.

"Hmm. Skeptical are we?"

Matt's big concern was the starter motor. It had taken several days of patient rebuilding after the meltdown. He hoped his repair worked. Spares for the thirty-year-old BMC diesel would be tough to find, and it would be a bitch sailing around here without an engine. He reconnected the newly charged battery, crossed his fingers and turned the key. "Damn!"

Chapter 21

Thelma rolled her eyes when Matt cussed. She knew the engine wouldn't start. She watched Matt run a series of complex circuit tests and refastened the battery terminals before he found the problem. In his hurry to get things running, he'd overlooked the obvious. The battery switch was still on CABIN, a battery long dead.

She couldn't help but giggle at his insistence to make things more difficult than they really were, an endearing trait reminiscent of her original owner.

Matt fixed Tune-up with a withering look. "Why didn't you point that out? It would've saved me a lot of messing around."

The cat looked away as if to say, *What did you expect, miracles?*

"You've gotta earn your keep around here, buddy. No free lunches."

This time when he turned the key, the engine responded with a healthy chant: Ra Ra Ra Ra. Matt gave his first mate a thumbs-up. "A touch of ether and I think she'll fly." He made sure the fuel tank selector was on the full tank, shot a half-second burst of starter fluid into the air filter and cranked the engine. Ra Ra Ra RRRRRUUUUMMMMMMMM.

The gauges snapped awake. The cat yawned.

The knockity ring of the diesel was an inspirational drum solo to Matt's ears. He yelled over the bluster of the iron genny. "All systems go, Mister Mate."

While the engine warmed up, he surveyed the anchorage, a sight that initially appeared a haven, but now felt like decayed urban sprawl. He lifted the cat to his chest and showed him the scene. "How about we find someplace rural."

That was the tune Thelma wanted to hear. She knew her captain was in a state of mind that left him vulnerable to rum shops and mischief ashore. "Hear that, Missy? Captain's canceled his shore leave. Prepare to make sail."

Theodora had been ecstatic about her engine coming to life, knowing her electrical system would soon have the power to bathe her in a glamorous light each night. But Matt's decision to leave had turned her temperate mood into a tempest. She stomped around the forward hatch, flinging her head of dark hair with each new expletive. She raved about the injustice of leaving her admirers and losing the attention she deserved.

Matt went forward to man the windlass. Tune-up followed. When he reached the forward hatch, he arched his back, clawed the air and spat.

Matt glanced around, wondering what might have incited his mate to get his hackles up. "What's with you? Thinkin' about that Frenchman?"

Thelma busied herself with a loose curler and quipped, "You've made a friend, Missy."

The queen leaned toward Tune-up, held out her own 'Aged Burgundy' claws and spat right back. "Don't you hiss at me, shark bait!" She stormed to her perch on the mast and sat in sulky gloom. After a moment, she eyed the jib halyard where it ran through a block at the top of the mast and an idea began to brew. Ha, she thought, we'll see who has the last laugh.

Matt cranked in the chain until *TR's* bow was directly over the anchor, then engaged the prop and powered the hook from the sand. Once he'd secured the anchor, he motored through the channel between St. Thomas and St. Johns.

Light, shifty winds teased the water. Mashed potato clouds seemed stuck to the sky. The dense boat traffic reminded him of Florida. He imagined the frustration of having to sail in such pitiful conditions and felt relieved to have a working engine again.

Several hours later, he was in waters claimed by the British Virgin Islands. South of Tortola he rounded a green, wooded point of land. Swirled turrets poking above a grove of dense hardwoods marked an opulent estate of pinkish stucco that covered the higher ground like a strawberry ice cream topping. His chart indicated deep water right to shore and, despite a light onshore breeze, the confidence he had in the motor enticed him to hug the rocky beach.

Thelma stood on the bowsprit, watching the land draw closer. She had been apprehensive since Matt motored from the harbor with sail covers on and the anchor in its chocks–not a single back up at the ready. Granted, her diesel was a dependable machine in most respects, but it still required the captain to see to its needs. Directing the fuel overflow to the proper tank was one of them, a simple twist of a valve that Matt had overlooked. But closing on an exposed headland under power with an onshore wind was plain foolhardy. She turned to Theodora who sat cross-legged on the forward hatch, mirror in hand. "I thought he'd know better than this," she told the queen. "Seems our Matt is determined to learn things the hard way."

Matt gave Tune-up's tail a light tug, then pointed at the pink house. "How would you like to live there? I'll bet you'd have your own personal cat-chef."

He took his mate's purr as an affirmative response.

"You can have it, Mister Mate. A life of leisure translates to boring for me. I'm quite content with *TR*."

The engine, which for hours hadn't skipped a beat, raced to a high scream then settled back to the normal revs.

A bucket of adrenaline splooshed into Matt's bloodstream. "What the?" He knew instantly the engine had sucked air, which meant he'd run out of fuel. He flicked open the latches on the engine hatch and lifted the lid. His hand shot to the tank selector and snapped it to the other tank. *Damn! Hope I caught it in time.*

The engine raced twice, stuttered and died.

Spinning the helm hard over, Matt hoped TR's momentum would carry her from the land, now only a stone's throw away. "Like I said," he told the cat, "nothing boring for me."

He tried to restart. All he got was a steady Ra Ra Ra. "Sucked too much air, buddy. Don't have time to bleed the system now. Let's get the sails up." Tune-up didn't lift a paw.

Matt scrambled to remove the mainsail cover, attach the halyard and raise the sail, but without a headsail *TR* refused to sail against the light wind. Her sideways drift forced her closer to shore. The steady drone of the diesel had lulled him into a false sense of security. "Nice move, Matthew," he muttered.

When he tried to raise the jib, the halyard jammed in the masthead block. "Shit!" No amount of tugging would free the line. Now he was so close he could see tiny crabs dodging the light surf on the shoreline rocks.

Thelma tossed her hands up and hissed in disgust. "Now he's got us in a fine mess. What I don't understand is how our jib halyard managed to kink in the block."

Theodora, strangely quiet, stared at the shrinking distance to shore. It didn't take Thelma long to equate the queen's silence to the trouble they were in. "Lord, Missy, you've got oakum for brains. We'd be safer with a Jonah aboard."

Theodora wore a poutish frown and wouldn't meet Thelma's gaze. "How was I to know we'd be sightseeing this close to shore? It was a prank, nothing more."

Thelma pointed to the rocks. "Have a good look at your prank, Missy. If we hit those, your pretty paint will be the least of our worries." This was the second time in as many weeks that the queen's actions had threatened their mutual interest of staying afloat. It seemed as though her royal brain was full of dry rot and the only fix for that was remove and replace. Thelma hadn't a clue as to how one would even begin the first step of removal, but she was a ready and willing replacement.

Matt abandoned the headsail idea and finally launched the anchor over the bow. Chain rattled over the roller with increasing speed as the heavy plow raced for the bottom. He set the brake when a hundred feet had run out. *TR* was less than fifty feet from shore.

He kept a hand on the chain and when he felt the first vibrations of the anchor touching ground, began to crank in the slack. The windlass pall tinked sharply against the gears, rapidly at first until he felt the plow bite. He watched over his shoulder as TR's stern swung toward the rocks. The dinghy, tailing behind, bounced off the nearest one.

Chapter 22

Porky wailed when his pontoons struck the barnacle-covered rocks. *TR's* stern bore down on him. Another few feet and he'd be squashed, ruptured, turned to flotsam on the beach.

Matt cranked in a few more feet. He held his breath. The chain stretched. *TR* came up hard on the anchor, hesitated, then pulled away from shore.

Tune-up rubbed against Matt's leg. He gave him a pat. "Yeah, I keep forgetting about Mr. Murphy's law."

Before Matt could lower the mainsail and tend to the engine, a beefy Asian guy in a gray security uniform, radio and nightstick dangling from his belt, strode from behind a thick clump of tropical greenery above the beach. A stressed-out Doberman whined and tugged on a short leash the man held in his left hand. Tune-up stiffened and a low yowl of warning, like a dying siren, came from his throat.

The guard made a shooing motion with his unoccupied arm. "Private property, skipper. Move along," he bellowed.

Matt chuckled to himself. It was obvious the guard was clueless about boats. No skipper in his right mind would be here on purpose. He stood on the stern and waited for the guard to reach the water's edge, then spoke. "Nice pooch."

No answer. Heavy frown.

"I appreciate your vote of confidence, but I've got a small engine problem. Only take a few minutes to fix."

"You've got five." Then he spoke into a hand-held radio.

How generous, Matt thought. Wonder what happens when my time's up. He suppressed a flippant retort and turned to the problem.

After dousing the main, he tackled the messy three-step procedure to get the air out of the fuel lines. The task was made worse by his stewing over the attitude of the guard. He glanced at the cat. "I'm having a hard time with the concept of paradise around here."

Tune-up scratched behind his ragged right ear as if to say, *Tell me about it.*

"It seems the Virgin Islands have turned into an archipelago of hard-core street walkers. I'm thinking of sailing to points south."

Tune-up shifted to his back and stretched. Matt took the action to say, *Fine by me.*

About the time air bubbles ceased to foam from the fuel line, Matt heard a large outboard approach, throttle back and die. *TR* rocked in the resulting wake. He lifted his head from the engine hatch to see what was going on.

A twelve-foot black Zodiac carrying two more guards had arrived. Both were muscular black guys in straining uniforms. One of them wore a blue knit cap. Cap yelled, "You were told to leave, skipper. What's the delay?"

Christ, what the hell is with these people? He couldn't hold his tongue. He raised his greasy hands. "Waiting for the kettle to boil. You boys care for a cup of tea?"

The two guards exchanged looks then deferred to the Asian guy standing with the dog on shore. The dog barked. The guard told the other two guys, "Help him out."

Matt had no desire for their help. He ducked down, tightened the fuel line connection, then grabbed up the can of starting fluid. Before he could prime the engine, Cap picked up an aluminum oar and with one hefty stroke, propelled the Zodiac against *TR's* hull.

Tune-up crouched beside the bulwarks.

The other guy reached for *TR's* rail.

As soon as his hand touched wood, Tune-up sprang, front paws a blur. The hand turned to hamburger. The guy screeched, jerked his hand back and shoved the Zodiac away.

Cap swung the oar at Tune-up. It sliced the air above the cat's head. Before he could swing again, Matt shot a stream of starting fluid at Caps face. The guy jerked up his arms against the spray, lost his balance and flipped over the side with a splash.

Matt lunged for the ignition switch. The engine cranked on and on. The dog went ballistic, howling and yapping. The Asian guy shouted something into his radio.

Matt gave the engine a quick shot of ether and it roared to life. He jammed the gearshift to forward, then powered into deep water, dragging anchor and chain. The Asian guard watched from shore, one fist on his hip. The guy with the mangled hand helped his buddy back into the Zodiac. Matt waved then cupped his hands around his mouth. "Have a great day!"

He motored a half-mile out until he was sure the guys in the Zodiac weren't going to follow then stopped to crank the anchor and chain aboard. Tune-up sat by the windlass and Matt reached out to ruffle his fur. "We make a good team, Mister Mate. Maybe we taught those guys some manners."

An hour later, he was in a secure anchorage in flat water over conch-grass and sand. It was a shallow cut on the west side of a small island protected by low rocky arms, no houses in sight. A small crowd of pasty-white people lounging in the cockpit of a glitzy charter yacht was his only company. Curious to know what had jammed the jib halyard block, Matt clipped the canvas bosun's chair and tool bucket to the main halyard, stepped into the chair, then hoisted himself, hand over hand, to the top of the mast. Huffing from the exertion, he tied himself off, thinking of the two cases of Coors in the bilge. A cool breeze dried the sweat on his face and chest. He took a moment to appreciate the view fifty-feet above the water.

Tune-up was a mere speck on the foredeck. The green lumps of the island chain lay scattered around the horizon, melting into the afternoon mist. Charter boats converged on popular watering holes, their clients probably thirsty for a sundowner. He returned a wave from one of his neighbors then turned his attention to the block.

One glimpse and he burst out laughing. Shaking his head in amazement, he wondered how the hell the halyard could have looped through the bottom of the bronze sheave. His earlier tugging had pulled the loop back through the top of the block, binding the line in a hopeless wrap. The physical laws that would allow this particular mess were beyond his understanding. He chalked it up to the Bermuda Triangle. It took him five minutes with a screwdriver to remove the sheave, untangle the knot and reassemble the block. The trip back to the deck would be his reward –an exhilarating rappel to a bilge-cool beer.

When his feet hit the deck, he could already taste the tang of a frothy brew. He wiggled from the chair, danced past the cat and swung down the companionway in single-minded pursuit of refreshment. He pried loose the middle board of the cabin sole and reached in to snag a can of Coors. The instant his fingers closed on the thin aluminum he knew something was wrong. He flashed on the recent flood in the bilge, the two cases of Coors bobbing in saltwater. His shoulders sagged and he slowly lifted a half-full can from the bilge. He held it to the light and squeezed. Chalky walls crumpled. Flat, stale beer oozed from dozens of invisible pinholes and ran down his arm. The bilge smelled like a roadside tavern on a Saturday night.

Matt looked at Tune-up who watched from the top of the companionway steps. "Don't laugh. This is a real tragedy."

He retrieved the remaining cans, hoping to find at least one that hadn't corroded through from the saltwater. No luck. With a sad shake of his head, he scooped the army of mortally wounded soldiers into a plastic trash bag and replaced the board. Then he stood and petted the cat. "Could be worse. Could be blood from my slashed wrists."

Chapter 23

At midnight the wind shifted in a raging squall. What was once a snug harbor became a deathtrap for any boat whose anchor couldn't hold. Thelma watched her anchor chain loop back on itself as her bowsprit swung, facing the open fetch to the west. She heard a loud "whoop" off her stern then the queen's mirthless laugh. The last gust had brought Porky up hard on his painter, snap-rolled him over and he now flopped around like a mackerel on the beach.

Thelma shot the queen a disgusted look. "It's no laughing matter. If you were worth your salt, you'd be more concerned with our own mooring." At that moment, the chain came taut and pitched the queen to her knees.

Thelma helped her to her feet. "You keep your eye on our anchor and holler if it drags. Our skipper's got a tempest to tame and might need my help."

Bleary eyed from a deep sleep, Matt hopped naked through the forward hatch and onto the deck. The rain stung like driven sand. He was instantly awake. With his back to the rain, he could just make out the dark loom of land off his stern.

Hysterical shouts came from the nearby boat; erratic flashlight beams cut the night. When the anchor chain jerked tight, he knelt and grabbed the chain and waited for the telltale vibration of an anchor skidding along the bottom, but the big plow held. Matt hustled to the cockpit and ducked below for his foul weather gear. Tune-up lay curled in a cozy corner under the spray dodger and Matt ruffled his fur on the way back out. "I've about had it with this place. How about you?"

He took a moment to haul the dinghy aboard and lash it to the cabin top then paused to consider his options. He could maybe ride it out, but the wind had a weight to it that implied long duration. It wouldn't be hard to pop around the headland and take shelter in the lee but it was rare to get a good wind from the west. Besides, once he reached Antigua the beat east would pretty much be over.

Thelma felt her bow rise to the increasing swell and hoped her captain had the sense to get clear of this lee shore. She watched Porky make his clumsy way forward to where the queen kept watch on the anchor.

Matt fired up the motor and left it to idle out of gear, then tucked a double reef in the mainsail and hoisted it up. As soon as he sheeted it home, *TR* sailed off on a port tack, coming up hard on her chain to cross the wind. While she tacked, Matt cranked in the slack with the windlass. It took six tacks before *TR* sailed over her anchor and pulled it from the muck below. Matt cranked madly on the winch handle. A four-foot swell now rolled into the anchorage and TR pitched sharply. The mud-laden anchor broke the surface, swung in a vicious arc and with a sickening thunk, gouged the hull.

Theodora threw her arm across her eyes and let out a shrill scream. "My planks, my planks!" She collapsed with a moan and muttered something about her lovely paint.

Tune-up snapped to his feet, arched his back and let out a long hiss, his good eye dilated.

Thelma, who'd watched Matt with approval, winced more from the scream than the actual damage. She knew about mishaps in difficult situations and carried the scars to prove it. She gave her prostrate eminence an impatient wave of her hand. "Lord, Missy, batten your hatch. Save the act for a real disaster."

Porky knelt by the queen's feet and stroked her ankle as though to impart comfort. "Don't worry," he said, "it's not so bad."

For a moment she indulged Porky's fetish, then sat up and slapped his hand away. "How would you know, barnacle brain, it's not even your hull. If we'd stay in a marina where I belong, this would never happen."

Thelma rolled her eyes and shuddered at the thought of congested life dockside where any number of close encounters could blemish her cosmetics.

Matt secured the anchor and moved cautiously back to the helm, berating himself for the ugly gash but concluded he was probably lucky to get away with just the one. He found Tune-up pacing in a tight circle under the dodger, his head twitching from side to side. "Relax buddy, I think we're under control."

Heeling to twenty knots of wind, he motorsailed into open waters, sheets of warm saltwater probing his foul weather gear for the slightest opening. He held course for what seemed hours, but was really thirty minutes, to clear the south end of the island then turned east for the downwind run to Antigua. Off the wind, without the motor, life was again a picnic. While he rigged the staysail and put Fred to work he reflected on the exhilarating extremes that made cruising life worth living and applauded, once again, his decision to sail the world.

In the forepeak, amidst a mountain of wet chain, Thelma and Porky struggled to console Theodora—she with patience and he with dim understanding. Her last tirade contained enough abrasive language to scrub the slime from a sea wall. In the ensuing silence they heard Tune-up yowling in the galley. Porky gave Thelma a plaintive look and she harumphed. "You've even got the cat upset, Missy. If I know our captain, we won't be sporting a bruise for long."

The queen jumped to her feet and thrust a long manicured nail at the cat. "Spare me the poor kitty's feelings. You're hacking up furballs as much as I am. And I've had it with your "working girl" crap."

At first, Matt couldn't figure out the whining he heard over the howling wind, but finally glimpsed Tune-up in the galley with his back arched, staring forward and realized it was cat noise. He crouched in the companionway. "What's up dude?"

Tune-up gave him a quick glance over his shoulder then snapped his head back. Puzzled, Matt dropped to the cabin floor and made his way to the galley. He knelt down and followed the cat's gaze. "What is it, bud?" Everything looked shipshape. Nothing out of place, no obvious leaks. He checked the bilge in case the goofy feline was trying to tell him they were about to sink. But no, just the usual puddle. He glanced again at the cat, which hadn't moved, and shrugged. "It's a mystery to me, guy." The episode made him wonder what he was missing. The cat obviously knew something he didn't and he hoped that whatever it was, wasn't important. Then again, maybe the cat was just a bit crazy.

Ever since the queen had admitted to knotting her halyard in the block at the top of the mast, Thelma had been in a quandary. It had become clear that what drove the queen to sabotage her own well being, and hence Thelma's and of course the captain's, was more than just a bit of malarkey. The she-devil had some punky wood in her topsides and Thelma still didn't know what to do about it. But as sure as there was copper in her bottom paint, she would come up with something.

The queen's reaction to the anchor gouge seemed totally out of proportion to the damage. Anyone with a normal sense of themselves could be reasoned with, but not the queen. From experience, Thelma knew she couldn't confront her without fear of some unforeseen backlash that would again endanger the ship and crew.

During their two-day sail to Antigua, Thelma pondered her options. The most drastic, of course, being getting rid of the queen entirely. But this solution involved challenges she felt were beyond her capabilities. For starters, she'd have to convince her captain to change the boat's name back to Thelma. How would she go about that? Those were uncharted waters indeed. She'd never had reason to make herself known to any of her captains and it had never occurred to her that she could. Furthermore, unlike the queen, she had no experience at this sort of skullduggery. If Theodora were to find out what she was up to she might just as well dash herself on some rocky shore as go to sea with a slighted queen. At least then her captain might survive.

The more reasonable approach would be to try and win the queen over through her vanity. Rather than confront her majesty at each turn maybe holding her no-nonsense tongue would smooth her royal tantrums, like rain on a rough sea.

Chapter 24

Theodora, mirror in hand, preened herself by the forward hatch as they entered the harbor at St. John's, Antigua. A cloudless sky gave the sun a harsh bite. Yachts and commercial vessels of all shapes and sizes swung at anchor. A massive white cruise ship dwarfed it all. She was in her element now, her aloof stance demanding recognition. Thelma, while keeping a weather eye for obstructions in the buoyed channel, stood beside the queen and patted her curlers in place.

If Theodora noticed this uncharacteristic action, she gave no hint. "I hope you're satisfied with your rolling waves and endless horizons for now, Thelma. I think our captain will find plenty of distractions ashore to make our stay here a long one."

As much as she loathed the thought, Thelma gave a slow nod. "You may be right Missy, our Matt deserves a bit of shore leave. And there is that nasty ding in our bow to repair."

At this, Theodora raised one eyebrow and glanced Thelma's way, but kept silent.

Tune-up sat beside the helmsman's seat, his raucous purr competing with TR's diesel.

Matt stood leaning on the boom with one foot on the seat and the other on the wheel as he wound his way into the inner harbor. The light prevailing wind carried a distinctive mix of smoldering coconut husk, diesel and low tide. "This is more like it, big guy. I think we crossed a magic line somewhere east of the Virgins. This place screams Caribbean." Since bailing out of their last anchorage Matt had taken to speaking more freely to the cat. It seemed to ease his sense of isolation as a singlehander. The solo sailing gig had never held much appeal for him, but the last couple of weeks had given him some insight to the lifestyle. There was something to be said for not having to share tight quarters or continually seek compromise. Mind you, there was a lot more to think about when getting under way, changing sails and anchoring. Each step had to be carefully considered or chaos would reign.

Thelma had watched with approval as Matt readied the anchor prior to reaching the congested area of the harbor. And now, as he conned TR into the anchorage, it was a simple matter to shift into reverse, walk to the bow and release the brake. Chain rattled out of the locker, the big plow hit sand and when Matt set the brake it dug in deep.

Much to the queen's dislike, her captain had chosen to anchor well out of the main channel amongst the local island riff-raff. A rusty interisland tramp and a few roughly planked fishing boats painted in violent hues of red, yellow and green were her closest neighbors. Theodora frowned into her mirror. "A lot of good our classic lines do when there's nobody around to appreciate 'em."

Well, I do, you vain hussy. "I'm sure he has his reasons. It's a calm anchorage for one and you know how much we like to roll."

"I don't mind a roll as long as we're in the spotlight."

"I rather fancy a bit of a roll, too, but our Matt doesn't. It's best you accept that, Missy. No good can come from crossing the captain."

Theodora grumbled something then retreated to her perch on the spreaders.

Matt ran up the yellow quarantine flag and pumped life back into Porky. Tune-up followed his moves with his one good eye. "Gotta clear in Mister Mate. You're in charge while I'm gone. Repel all boarders and stay sober." With that he hoisted the dinghy over the side, climbed in and rowed off.

Porky waved to the two ladies, only one of which returned the gesture.

While not all that picturesque, St. John's was a hub of commerce and the place teemed with activity. Random shouts, the whine of scooters and blaring music from seaside rum shops kept the island pulse alive. There was no shortage of bright paint and Porky felt like he truly belonged. Tender to a queen and world travel—what else could a boy want?

The clearing in formalities were just that, a formality. Matt wandered the streets of the capital before settling in at an Internet café advertising cold Wadadli beer. E-mails awaited and as he sucked down his first taste of the Windward Islands he composed a brief account of his weeks alone. No doubt all his friends and family were well aware of Sara's return.

Matt spotted his reflection in a storefront window and barely recognized the hairy countenance staring back. "Lookin' a bit rough there, Mathew," he mumbled. It didn't take him long to find a barbershop and have his wavy locks and full beard trimmed.

Thirty minutes later and feeling five pounds lighter he replenished his cash at an ATM, picked up fresh produce and cold *bottled* beer at a market near the harbor and rowed home.

After the near theft of his dinghy in St. Thomas, Matt decided to hoist Porky on deck at night while in crowded places.

Thelma gave Porky a pat on the cheek. "Isn't this a delight? We'll have a grand time swapping yarns or maybe a hand of gin rummy or two."

Theodora, though still in a funk about her low-life neighbors, beckoned to the boy. "You might as well join the party, you're as much flash as were going to get around here."

Porky sat beside the queen on the foredeck and leaned against the mast. "The big cruise ship is called *Sea Princess.* Is she related to you?"

Theodora flinched at the question and Thelma expected a sharp sassy reply, but the queen surprised her. "No. There were no heirs to my throne."

Thelma watched a wave of emotion cross the queen's face. *Pain? Regret? Sadness? Definitely some ugly history there.*

The next day Matt got out a can of Bondo. Working from the dinghy, he filled and fared the deep gouge made by the anchor.

Theodora could almost forgive him her isolation when he carefully laid on a fresh coat of paint that made the wound disappear.

"Didn't I tell you our Matt would take care of that in Bristol fashion? He's not one to let things slide."

"Shut your porthole, Thelma. I can see he's got my interest at heart. Let's just hope it stays that way."

Thelma could only shake her head at that and pity any female companions her captain might bring aboard.

After a long night of three-handed gin rummy—a game Porky took to like a pro and flustered the two ladies—the captain called all hands. The clankity clank of the anchor windlass roused Tune-up. He leapt from his berth under the dodger and trotted forward to rub against Matt's leg.

"Mornin', Mister Mate. Prepare to make sail, we have a favorable wind and there's not a moment to lose."

Once TR had shortened up on her anchor, Matt cranked over the diesel, raised the main then brought the big plow home. "We're headed for English Harbor, home of Lord Nelson's dockyard," he told Tune-up. The big cat's purr surpassed the diesel. "Should be there by lunchtime if this wind holds."

When Thelma heard that last phrase she spoke to the queen. "There he goes, tempting fate with landfall predictions. I'd bet the bronze in our fastenings it'll be suppertime before the anchor is down."

Theodora harrumphed. "Makes no difference to me as long as it's somewhere other than here. Even a dockyard sounds exciting compared to this slum."

"You'll get your share of oglers at Nelson's, Missy. I was there with the colonel a few years back and the place is gunnel to gunnel with fancy yachts from around the world."

The queen was all smiles. "Sounds like my kind of place, and about time, too."

Admittedly, Thelma had enjoyed her time with the colonel back then. He'd been a real naval history buff and Nelson's dockyard was a highlight for him. Antigua had always been the hub for the British navy in the Caribbean. With its strategic location and multiple fine harbors, the island had no equal. Being British born and bred, Thelma had felt right at home, the English oak in her timbers exuding tradition with every growth ring. But now that *Theodora R* was on the transom, she wasn't sure how she'd feel.

It had been well over a century since the great ships of the line plied these waters and Nelson's dockyard had slowly evolved from a working shipyard into a modern-day marina with all the expected conveniences.

Under full sail, with Fred steering a southerly course, *TR* reached the southwest corner of Antigua before 9 a.m. The moderate breeze from the northeast held steady, but now a steep southeast swell rolled in from the open Atlantic. When Matt changed course for the east leg of the trip *TR* met the waves head on. Her speed launched her off the crest of one wave smack into the face of the next bringing her to a near standstill. Green water cascaded down the deck.

Theodora clutched the mast, cringing with fear, water up to her ankles.

Porky sat bouncing on his inflated bow, a wide grin lighting up his face.

Thelma kept a steady hand on the bow rail. "Don't worry Missy, we can handle these seas, but our Matt better shorten sail soon or I fear for our big genny."

Matt, realizing the need for the high-cut working jib up forward put the helm hard over, but *TR* was slow to turn. The next bow wave tossed a massive wall of water into the foot of the genny. The strained dacron parted with a sharp crack.

Theodora screamed.

Thelma hit the deck.

Porky let out a "Yeow!"

Tune-up dove down the companionway.

Chapter 25

Matt felt the shock in his legs. The wild flapping of shredded sail drowned out his curses. He brought the bow around and retreated to the sheltered side of the island.

Thelma couldn't fault her skipper. He'd made the right moves but the sea had caught him with a parting shot over the bow. She watched with approval as Matt wasted no time switching sails, careful to clip himself in when out on her bowsprit.

The sun had just kissed the horizon as *TR* sailed into Falmouth harbor, a mile short of their intended destination. The wide-open circular bay was an inviting anchorage and Matt dropped the hook among dozens of other sailboats taking advantage of the protected waters. A network of jetties extended out from the head of the bay where the moneyed yachts lived.

As soon as the queen spotted the sailing crowd, she quickly forgot her fears of the day. In no time at all she was properly primped for the royal welcome.

The short eastern slog had taken far longer than Matt had anticipated and he was glad to be riding on quiet water. English Harbor could wait.

"Suppertime," Thelma said. "Didn't I tell you? *If this wind holds* are four words a sailor should never say aloud—guaranteed to wreak havoc at sea."

"Get over it, you old salt. Time for us to shine. Let's forget about the last eight hours. I can already feel the admiring eyes."

Unlike Florida and the Virgin Islands where fleets of Tupperware boats were the norm, Falmouth hosted a vast array of traditional sailing craft, from gaff-rigged schooners to simple sloops. Polished bronze and varnished spars were on parade and the queen felt she was finally consorting with others of her station.

Tune-up sensed the change in Theodora's demeanor and paced the decks with a content rumbling purr.

Matt was below, challenging his culinary skills with a recipe for mac and cheese when a sharp knock sounded on the hull followed by a gruff "Ahoy, *Theodora R.*"

When he climbed into the cockpit he found a bearded, sunbaked stick figure standing in a small wooden rowing pram, one hand on *TR's* gunnel, the other scratching the cat behind the ears. "I'm Per, off the *Brindle*." He pointed to a sleek white yawl, flying a Danish flag. "I watched you sail in and thought I recognized the boat, but I guess not. You're not the fellow I met last year."

Matt extended his hand. "Name's Matt, and you're right, we haven't met, but I recently bought this boat from Colonel Stockton. Her name used to be *Thelma*."

Per's face lit up. "I knew it. Yes, I knew the colonel—admired the boat."

"C'mon aboard. Got some cool beer in the bilge."

Per shrugged. "Why not? Sun's over the yardarm." He tied off his dinghy, climbed with alacrity into the cockpit and settled on a cushioned seat.

Thelma smiled. She remembered Per from the year before. Being of similar age, he and the colonel had hit it off. They'd spent hours aboard each other's vessels, spinning yarns and one-upping each other into the night.

Matt ducked below, snagged two beers from the bilge, popped the caps and handed one to his guest. "Cheers. Or should I say skoal?"

"Cheers works. Thank you." Tune-up leapt to his berth under the dodger. "Your first mate looks like a brawler."

Matt laughed. "He's got his rough side but earns his keep."

"I must ask why you changed the name. In Denmark this can be very bad luck."

The queen scowled at this. "What business is it of his?"

Thelma looked askance at Theodora. "It's obvious he's concerned for our captain's well being, which is more than I can say for some."

"I got rid of Sara, didn't I? We'd have been second chariot with her at the helm. *Give the poor girl a chance* is all I heard from you."

Matt gave his stock answer. "Thelma didn't instill the confidence I wanted for a circumnavigation."

Per gave a slow nod. "How's the trip been so far? Smooth sailing?"

He's got me there. "Outside of my girlfriend abandoning ship in mid-ocean, almost sinking the boat, being overrun with roaches and unexplained rigging issues, yeah, it's been smooth sailing."

Both men burst out laughing.

"That's all I need," the queen snapped. "Someone questioning the captain's good judgment."

Thelma kept a straight face but couldn't help thinking that was *exactly* what she needed.

"In my own defense," Matt said. "I'm still a bit green at the cruising life. In fact I'd planned to put in at English Harbor, but blew out my jenny in the big swell out there."

"It's well you put in here. Antigua charter week started yesterday and every charter boat in the Windwards is tied up in there. I doubt a kayak would find room."

"Must be quite a party."

"More rum than water and it's all free." Per tilted his head back, took a swig and gave Matt a wink. When he set his beer down he wasn't smiling. "Reason I ask about the name is because my grandfather was a fisherman all his life, long before diesel engines. He had a gift some would call a curse—a sense of the spirit world."

Thelma glanced up the mast and wondered if the queen, who had retreated to her perch on the spreaders, was listening in.

Matt settled back to listen.

"One of the first boats he crewed on was plagued with poor catches and trouble with nets and rigging after losing a man at sea. This man had a wife and small child who depended on him, but the captain of the boat did nothing to help. Grandfather felt the angry spirit of the man and knew this was the problem. He convinced the captain to deliver a basket of fish to the widow each time they returned to port and soon their luck changed.

"Word spread through the fleet and over the years Grandfather was called to purge all manner of demons. I have read his journals, and by far the most common cause of bad luck aboard ship was a change in the ship's name. Name changes did not always bring bad luck if they were done properly."

"What does properly mean?"

"His journals say that great care must be taken to insure there is no conflict between the spirits that the names possess. If the new name is chosen wisely, it generates good feelings between spirits."

"I've only considered a boat spirit to be nothing more than a silly superstition. And I definitely didn't look for any conflict between *Thelma* and *Theodora R.*" Matt ducked below for two more beers. He handed one to Per. "I take it you believe in this stuff. Do you have any personal experience with conflicting spirits?"

"For myself, no. I have had only this one boat, *Brindle*, and I had her built by a yard in Denmark. But when I was a teenager my father bought a used trawler named *Torden*. This means thunder in Danish. He didn't change the name but always there is trouble with the engine and leaks in the hull. He had to keep it in a shallow berth because it would sink. After he sells this boat for a big loss he finds out the original name was *Solskin* which means sunshine." Per laughed and slapped a bony knee. "My father never read his father's journals, but I did. It was easy for me to see a problem with the new name."

"That's it? Just the one instance?"

"With my family, yes. But I always ask about this when I hear of a new name for a boat. I hear both good and bad stories. I don't have my grandfather's gift, but I am always curious."

"Well, so far my trip hasn't exactly been a dream cruise," Matt said, 'but I have nothing to compare it to. For all I know everyone sailing has their share of trouble. And I wouldn't have the slightest idea how find out if there's a conflict between *Thelma* and *Theodora R.*"

The queen appeared by Thelma's side. "If that meddling bitch, Sara, hadn't interfered and let Matt cover your name, there would be no conflict."

"Heard that did you? A simple change of letters on our transom would do the same."

"In your dreams, you old scow. You heard the captain—I give him confidence."

Mercy, how can she live with herself? The acid on her tongue is enough to corrode bronze. She's the showboat and I'm the sailor and we'll never be kindred spirits.

Per scratched at the label on his beer bottle, then looked up. "Surely you know Theodora, you chose the name. If you find out who Thelma was, you have the answer."

Oh, you sweet man. Thelma wanted to give Per a big hug.

Matt thought for a moment. "With a little digging I'm sure I could come up with something. The colonel might even know."

Thelma's heart soared on a wave-crest.

The queen was strangely silent.

Per handed Matt his empty. "Thanks, I'll be on my way." He climbed into his dinghy and rowed off.

Giving a deep sigh, Matt shook his head and stroked the cat. "I think our buddy Per's been spending too much time in the sun without a hat. All that talk of spirit worlds, he'd do well as a Witness."

Thelma's heart washed up on a rocky shore and a tear ran down her cheek. She heard the queen's taunting laugh.

Chapter 26

Without sunglasses, Matt figured he'd be blind by now. Even still, the sun's reflection off the hundreds of square feet of brightly varnished teak made him squint. Mega-yachts from around the world were tied stern-to along the dockyard walls and beckoned with lavish pride. Not a line out of place, not a smudge on white fenders or the merest speck of tarnished brass was in evidence. Only 10 a.m. and folks in blue polo shirts, white duck trousers and boat shoes had already invaded the place, many brandishing a plastic cup of their favorite rum drink.

He'd started his tour with the 150-footers and was now down to those under 50. Despite the fact that Matt, dressed in baggy shorts, T-shirt and flip-flops, had no potential as a prospective charter guest, he felt welcome aboard even the most palatial yachts. He'd already declined three offers of rum punch.

As he strolled through the manicured grounds of the restored navy yard, he couldn't help wishing he'd had the landscape contract. The splash of colored blossoms and lush green on a palate of stone and timber construction were all contained by the high ground surrounding English Harbor—a landscaper's dream.

A cluster of classic sailboats caught his eye. As he came closer one in particular stood out. Something about the sweep of her decks, clipper bow and rake of twin spars set her apart. When he could see the wineglass transom, it read *Shanella,* and underneath, Boston. A full tan awning covered the teak decks and shaded the cockpit. A spry older guy with curly white hair dressed in khaki shorts and blue polo was helping an overweight woman climb up the companionway.

"Watch your step now," he said. "It's a ways down to the cockpit floor." A few grunts and groans ensued before the woman clutched the wheel and was steady on her feet.

A moment later a man—Matt assumed it was her husband—huffed from below. He extended his hand to White Hair. "Thanks for the tour, Captain." He took the proffered brochure and the couple wobbled up the gangplank to where Matt stood.

White Hair beckoned to Matt. "Come aboard."

Matt shucked the flip-flops and joined the captain. "Gorgeous boat. Spectacular curb appeal."

White Hair laughed. "Credit goes to Francis Herreshoff. He designed her and a yard in Maine built her."

"And you coddle her. Name's Matt, off the *Theodora R*. I'm anchored over in Falmouth."

"Bill Sykes." They shook hands and he waved Matt to a seat. "Didn't think you were charter material, but feel free to look around."

Up close, Bill's face had the weather wrinkles that spoke of serious sea time. Brown eyes were mere slits behind droopy lids. "Been doin' this long?" Matt asked.

Bill nodded. "Tenth season. Don't really need to be here for charter week, but the outfit that books most of my charters thinks it a good idea. Most of my clients are returns."

Matt surveyed the deck. "Must be close to fifty feet here. Are you on your own?"

"Just me most of the time. If I think I might need help with certain guests, my daughter flies in to crew. She's here helping me now but I sent her out to round up lunch."

He waved toward the companionway. "Have a look below. Got her all spiffed up for this show."

Matt climbed below to a forest of varnished hardwood. His eye was drawn to a stunning seascape of breaking waves on a rocky shore hung on the forward bulkhead. A spacious U-shaped settee around a gimbaled teak table sat to port and a brushed stainless galley to starboard. A modern navigation station was tucked into a snug quarterberth. Up forward were two roomy cabins, each with their own head and shower. He never felt the need to duck.

"Nice digs," he said, looking up at Bill. "But how do you manage to take care of all that stuff, sail the boat and run a charter by yourself? I'm singlehanding on thirty-five feet and have my hands full."

Bill handed Matt one of his brochures and pointed to the heading. It read, The Sailing Experience. "That's the secret. When you charter *Shanella* you learn to sail, cook, varnish wood and perform all basic boat maintenance."

"Ahh, the Tom Sawyer approach. I like it."

"Works for me," Bill said with a wink.

Just then, a woman appeared at the gangway with an armful of to-go containers. She wore a yellow tank top over teal capris on a lithe athletic body. Layered black hair cupped an oval face set off by soft Asian eyes. Matt guessed her to be in her early thirties. She kicked off a pair of slip-ons, exposing hot pink toenails.

"Found some awesome barbeque, Dad." She ducked under the awning and came up short. "Oh, sorry, didn't see we had a guest."

Matt climbed back to the cockpit. "No problem, I was just on my way. Your dad caught me admiring the boat."

"You aren't the first," she said. A wide smile showed lovely teeth.

"My daughter, Shanna. Shanna, Matt, he's anchored over in Falmouth. Bill reached down and lifted a hinged table into place.

His daughter set the containers down. "Don't run off, there's plenty if you'd like to join us."

"Please," Bill said. "I need a break from the sales pitch."

Matt got a whiff of the barbeque and his stomach gave an audible growl. He looked down. "I guess that cinches it."

Chapter 27

During the captain's absence a number of folks from neighboring boats passed close to *TR* on their way to shore. Once again the queen reveled in the spotlight. She was enthralled by the admiring comments, though she wasn't so sure about the 'salty old thing' voiced by two separate oglers. She noticed Thelma hadn't taken offence.

"Well, Missy, are you getting your fill?"

"Don't expect me to believe you don't like it, too, Thelma. I saw you trying to get yourself in ship shape. How do you like being called a salty old thing?"

Thelma clasped her hands against her chest. "Makes my old timbers swell with pride. Means we're meant for sailing the seas, Missy."

"I suppose you think that's a good thing."

Thelma stood tall. "Of course! Have a look at yourself. These doubled oak frames and thick planks beg for action. Our fastenings still have plenty of life. We can handle whatever seas our captain chooses to take on."

Theodora threw up her arms. "You are so...so...working class!"

Thelma smiled at the compliment.

The clatter of oars being shipped announced the captain's return. He tied off Porky and climbed aboard. Tune-up was on deck to greet him.

Matt rolled the cat to his back for a belly rub, eliciting a generous purr. "Miss me, big guy? I brought you a treat." Matt reached in his pocket and pulled out a plastic bag with two meaty ribs left from lunch. "For you, compliments of a very sweet lady."

Tune-up grabbed both offerings in his mouth and hopped down to a shady corner of the cockpit, where he commenced to chow down.

"You'll have to be on your best behavior tomorrow Mister Mate. She's coming aboard for a look-see. I think you'll like her. Knows her way around boats. Makes her living as an artist in

Mystic, Connecticut. I saw one of her paintings and she's quite talented. We have some work to do. I don't mind the lived-in look, but we can't have sloppy."

Thelma turned to the queen. "Sound's like our captain found himself a friend."

"Just what he needs, another distraction. Let's hope it's temporary."

"Don't be so hasty to judge, Missy. You heard him, we're bound to get our bronze shined. And she knows her way around boats."

"Whatever that means."

"You're a fine one to talk, with your knowledge of seamanship, or lack thereof."

"Stow it, Thelma. We're still afloat."

No thanks to you. "All I'm saying is we need to keep an open mind."

"Oh, I'm all for open-mindedness—as long as no one tries to change it."

Thelma rolled her eyes.

Matt hauled the blown jenny from the forepeak and set up the sewing machine on the dinette. Tune-up, having feasted, watched from the companionway. "First things first, big guy. We might have a steep learning curve with this project. I'm not exactly a seamstress and I've never used a hand-crank machine before."

Two hours later, after clearing a jammed bobbin for the umpteenth time, Matt's curses drove the cat into hiding. Frustrated with his dismal progress—one foot of stitching on eight feet of tear—Matt stuffed the sail back in its bag and stowed it forward. Tune-up peered down from the forward hatch. "Safe to come out now, buddy. It's beer-thirty and we can swab the decks and slap a coat of varnish on that hatch cover tomorrow."

He reclined in the cockpit with a cool brew and watched a sloop silhouetted by the setting sun sail into the harbor. Thoughts of the pleasant lunch he'd shared with Shanna and Bill were adrift in his mind when a dog's sharp bark brought him back to the now. As the sloop neared, Matt could make out the shapes of two dogs on the bow. He ducked below for the binoculars then focused on the boat. As it made its way past him, working toward the head of

the harbor he could just make out the French flag and the name:
Cher.

Chapter 28

Slowly lowering the binocs, Matt turned toward the cat. "The neighborhood just took a turn for the worse. Our French friend just cruised into town, big guy. We better get Porky out of harm's way."

As soon as Porky hit the foredeck Thelma called him over to the engine room where she and the queen waited with a deck of cards.

"Looks like you'll be with us for the night, lad. She shuffled and dealt three hands. "We have our honor to win back, you rascal."

Theodora eyed him with suspicion. "What other secrets are you hiding from us? If you'd pulled that stunt at my court I'd have fed you to the lions."

Porky, still unsure of how to take the queen, threw up both hands and vigorously shook his head. "No! No! No secrets your high…highness. I'm just good with numbers. I can remember all the cards."

Theodora leaned toward Thelma and whispered, "He's sharper than I gave him credit for. Good thing we're not playing for money."

Thelma gave the queen a cross look. "Don't pay your highness here any mind. She's a sore loser. But now that we know what we're up against, it won't as easy as last time for you to polish our prop."

Porky gave the queen an uneasy look, then picked up his cards. As soon as he fanned out his hand, a smile stretched across his face.

By daybreak, the queen had been thoroughly trounced. Porky tried to keep his giggles to a minimum. Thelma had held her own but worried about Theodora's funk. A sulking queen could mean serious mischief and she wasn't sure how to turn that tide.

As soon as the captain opened a can of varnish, however, that potential problem disappeared. Theodora threw in her hand. "I have more important things to attend to." She hovered over the forward hatch where Matt had wiped down the dull sheen of the old finish and was beginning to brush on a new glossy coat.

Tune-up, lying beside the anchor windlass, followed the queen's movements with his good eye. His purr turned into to a low growl.

Theodora hissed back and flashed her oxblood nails.

Matt looked up at the obvious change and took a look around the anchorage. "What's up? You smell our buddy with the dogs?" He noticed the cat seemed to be focused on something aboard, especially when he swiped a clawed paw through the air above his head.

"Hey, what's got into you? Too much barbeque?" Matt shrugged it off—*must have been a fly or something*—and continued painting.

By noon, Matt had scrubbed the decks and neatly coiled all the lines. He'd even run a polishing cloth over any spotted stainless and bronze. Theodora was in an absolute swoon.

Thelma even had a peek in the queen's mirror when she wasn't looking. She was feeling pretty good about herself and switched out the three-strand nylon rope she used to tie her robe for a colorful piece of polyester yacht braid.

The change didn't go unnoticed. "Well, aren't you the fancy one now. Nice to see you're finally getting with the program, Thelma."

Blushing, Thelma patted her curlers. "I'm not opposed to change, Missy, and I'll be the first to admit I like the extra care our captain takes with our appearance. The colonel felt a high shine was a waste of time and I was happy to go along with it. This dress-up takes a little getting used to."

The queen stepped close and ran an apprising eye from head to toe. "A little nail polish and lip gloss would go a long way to bringing out the real you."

Thelma's hand shot up defensively. "Not so fast, Missy. I can handle the trim of my own sails. I won't let myself look like some dockside whore just so someone will admire the cut of our jib."

Theodora gave a disgusted snort, whirled and stomped off.

As arranged, Matt rowed in to pick up Shanna. On his way he passed by the Frenchman's boat. Still wearing skimpy swim trunks, he was cleaning dog poop off the port side deck. His arm still sported a bandage. On the foredeck, the fiberglass dinghy Matt had seen him using in St. Thomas was fixed upside down as a makeshift kennel, where the two dogs hid from the sun. But tied astern was what tweaked Matt's interest—a new-looking, white inflatable dingy with attached 4hp Yamaha outboard. Matt couldn't help but think there was a cruiser out there missing his tender. He understood the unique position he was in concerning the possible theft, but wasn't sure what to do about it. After a moment's contemplation he tabled it for later. Right now he had something extremely pleasant on his mind.

Chapter 29

Today she wore tight navy shorts that highlighted shapely legs. A maroon tank top and white visor left a lot uncovered. She slipped off her sandals, much to Porky's relief, and hopped in like she'd always done it. Her toenails matched the maroon top. "You're by far the best looking thing I've seen today."

She laughed, her smile beaming. "You obviously haven't been off your boat."

"Well... no, but there are plenty of bikinied babes afloat out here." He rowed a few strokes then nodded at her toes. "I hope you didn't do that just for me."

She gave him an aloof look. "No, I did that in deference to the lady I'm about to meet. You said she had oxblood sails. This is the closest color I had."

"I'm sure she'll be impressed."

Shanna scanned the anchorage. "I was on Antigua last year for the event, but I never made it over to Falmouth. There must be over a hundred boats in here."

"One twenty-four was my closest count."

"Seriously, you counted them?"

"Doesn't take much to entertain me."

"I'll say." Matt noticed her focus suddenly shift to the Frenchman's boat. "Hey, René, *se va?*" she called, adding a hearty overhead wave.

Stunned, Matt stopped rowing and watched as René returned her wave and yelled back, "*Oui, se va.* Are you with your father again?"

No, Matt thought, *she's with me, turkey.*

As they drifted further with the wind Shanna cupped her hands around her mouth and shouted, "Yeah, same place, come visit."

René gave a thumbs-up and watched as Matt began rowing again.

Caught off guard, Matt came out with, "You know that guy, huh?"

Shanna laughed. "Duh, we met this time last year pretty much like you and I met. Only he didn't get any ribs."

"What do you know about him?"

She shrugged, "Not much, except his entire wardrobe seems to consist of skimpy swim trunks and his favorite subject is his canine companions. But I have to admit; I love the French accent. Why the interest?"

Matt waffled a moment, not wanting to label the guy a thief, just yet. "We've more or less crossed paths, but I'm not sure what to make of him. He didn't seem all that friendly."

"He was nice enough to me last year, but then again he probably thinks I'm better looking than you." She laughed, then scanning the anchorage asked, "Which one is the *Theodora R?*"

Glad to have the subject changed, Matt looked over his shoulder. "The one with the double spreaders and diamond rigging aloft."

The distinctive rig was easy to spot, and as they drew closer the hull came into view.

"Wow, that is one salty old girl. What a beaut. Love the bowsprit."

Rowing along side, Matt patted the hull. "Yeah, they don't come much saltier."

Tune-up's big head appeared over the gunnel.

"Whoa, this must be the mate." Shanna stood in the dinghy and reached a hand to pet the cat.

Matt was about to give warning but the raucous purr cancelled the need. "Yup, that's Tune-up, first mate and all around watch cat. He signed himself on a week ago when I was in St. Thomas."

"Sounds like a story in itself. He sure is big. I wouldn't want to mess with him."

"From the sound of things, I don't think that will be an issue."

Once aboard, Shanna walked the wide decks with her newest conquest. Matt watched her from the cockpit. Despite her sunglasses, he could tell by the way her gaze seemed to connect the dots, that she had a critical eye and understood what she was looking at. He called to her. "I can offer you a bilge-cool local brew."

She was bent over inspecting the anchor windlass. "Sure."

The two spirits watched Shanna's every move. Thelma was the first to speak. "I believe this gal knows what she's about, Missy. And I hope you noticed her nail polish is a close match to yours."

Theodora held out her hand, admiring her own nails. "No denying she has good taste. But does her interest lie with our captain or with us?"

"In all fairness, don't you think it's a mite too early to tell? We needn't jump to conclusions. For all we know we'll never see her again."

"Are you kidding? He's eyeing her like my eunuchs used to watch me bathe."

Shanna completed the topside tour and sat in the cockpit. She reached over and gave a sheet winch a spin. Matt handed her up a beer. "I'm impressed, but your description yesterday didn't do her justice."

"So you reckon she's more than a working class yacht?"

"Oh, yeah. She oozes integrity. Built in '36 you said, so she's what? Seventy-seven years old and just as honest as the day she was launched. Can I have a look below?"

Matt backed away from the companionway. "Be my guest."

Clutching the hatch cover she swung to the cabin sole rather than use the ladder and glanced around. "Look at the room in here. It's more like a forty-five footer. She ran her hand over the teak door to the quarterberth. The joinery puts *Shanella's* to shame. But don't tell my dad I said that."

Matt opened the back of the settee, exposing ample storage and the heavy oak frames of her hull. "Double sawn 4x4 oak frames every fourteen inches."

"Yikes, must be a whole tree here. She was clearly built for the heavy north seas."

"That I was, you angel," Thelma said.

The queen was over the moon from Shanna's caress and compliment to her teak door.

Pointing to the sewing machine on the table Shanna asked, "You do your own sail repair?"

He laughed. "I try, but so far the machine is winning."

"I know how that goes, but if you'd like a hand with it, I'm your gal."

"Thanks, I'll keep it in mind." He moved aside so Shanna could walk forward into the galley and the forward stateroom. He reached out and lifted the galley seat into place. "This is one of my favorite features."

She sat, bracing a knee against a lower cabinet. "This is too much. I'd love to feel secure cooking. I have to wear a harness in *Shanella* if we cook at sea. But that doesn't happen often." She ducked and moved forward so she stood under the open hatch. The cat watched her from the deck. Matt saw her eyes focus on the carved deck beam, then she pointed. "What's this, Matt?"

"Her original name and registration number." He went on to tell her about keeping it as an historical reference.

"So *you* changed the name?"

"Uh, yeah." He explained about his lack of confidence with the name Thelma.

Shanna sat quietly, head tilted as if listening to something, until Tune-up spat and clawed the air above her. She looked up in surprise. "Hmmm, that's interesting."

"He does that now and then, it's like he's got DT's and he's hallucinating."

Shanna ran her hand over the carved beam, feeling the letters and numbers. "At the risk of sounding a little woo-woo here, your first mate might be trying to tell you something."

Matt huffed a laugh. "What, like the boat's haunted?"

She merely shrugged. "I don't know, maybe something like that. Cats are fairly perceptive creatures."

The queen stomped her feet and shook her fist, causing the cat to react again. "I knew it. She's nothing but trouble. You heard the captain, he wanted confidence in his boat and she's just trying to undermine his decision."

Thelma held her tongue and crossed her fingers. *Could be the sunshine after the storm.*

Leading the way back to the cockpit, Matt spoke over his shoulder. "This is sounding a lot like old Per in the Danish boat next to us. He stopped by when we first came in...."

When he'd finished his story they were on their second beer and Matt had made popcorn. He'd shown the info describing Queen Theodora to Shanna, who seemed rather appalled. "So,

Matt, are you going to find out who Thelma was, look for a conflict?"

"I'd already blown it all off as so much bullshit, but here it comes again—getting kinda hard to ignore." He took a long pull from his beer. "It's obvious you like sailing. How come you're not full time on *Shanella*? No shortage of seascapes living on a boat."

She laughed. "Clearly, you've never chartered. It's like running a small hotel 24/7. I don't mind helping now and then but that's not for me. I told Dad if he ever wanted to do a circumnavigation I'd sign on in a heartbeat. But he's quite content with poking around the Caribbean."

"So no real ties to Mystic?"

"What do you mean by ties?"

"You know... home ownership, pets, relationships."

She smiled, showing lots of teeth. "I lease a condo that doesn't allow pets and no, I don't have a boyfriend right now."

Matt laughed to cover his blush. "I admit, I was curious."

"And you."

"Just me and the cat. But I didn't start out that way."

"I noticed you're not really set up for singlehanding. Looks to me like you have to leave the cockpit to do almost anything."

"If you're interested I can bore you with details."

"I'm all ears."

Chapter 30

"That's not an uncommon story in the cruising world. But the jumping ship mid ocean is a first. Good thing you weren't married. I have a girlfriend who experienced things from Sara's side and she's been dealing with a long distance divorce for over a year—total pain in the ass."

Matt laughed. "I guess that's the bright side."

Shanna looked toward the setting sun. "I have to be getting back. Dad and I are entertaining some prospective clients tonight and I'm the sous chef."

On the row to shore Shanna removed her sunglasses and Matt couldn't help but stare.

"What?" she said, clearly at a loss.

"Where did you get those eyes?"

"Oh brother, are you ever a hopeless romantic. These were a gift from my Japanese mother." Her face turned somber. "She died when I was eighteen."

He reached out and touched her knee. "I'm sorry."

She smiled again. "Thanks, but Dad and I moved on a long time ago. But I do commune with her now and then."

'Well, the next time you commune with her, tell her I love the eyes."

"Will do." She picked up her sandals and clambered ashore. "Thanks for a great afternoon. It wasn't without surprises. I'll be in touch."

"Look forward to it." As he rowed back to *TR* Matt noticed René watching him from the deck of *Cher*. He couldn't help thinking the guy must know it was *TR's* dinghy he'd tried to steal in St. Thomas. *But does he know that I know?*

Aboard the *Theodora R* a hurricane brewed. "That miserable feline has it in for me and I'm a bad enemy to have." The queen kept up a steady rant as she stalked the decks, using what worldly powers she had to intimidate the first mate. Wherever Tune-up settled she was there to let loose a lashed section of canvas or pull tight a coil of line his paw may have rested on. When he curled up

126

in the cockpit she eased the cleated topping lift until the bitter end slipped through and the boom fell with a resounding crash. Only a slight deflection off the ships wheel prevented the loss of one of his nine lives.

Thelma wasn't powerless to stop her, but chose to give Theodora all the scope she needed to run herself aground. *Maybe I won't even have to participate in her demise.*

When Matt returned, Tune-up, in an agitated state, leapt into Porky before Matt had tied him off. "What's with you, buddy?" And then he noticed the boom lying across the cockpit combing. He hoisted himself aboard and had a look around. His neatly coiled lines were now in disarray, the mainsail cover flapped in the breeze and one cockpit cushion lay on the floor. He looked back at the cat, sitting calmly in the dinghy. "What the hell's got into you? How did you drop the boom? Are you trying to tell me you need time ashore? Can it wait till morning?"

Matt hopped into the dinghy and lifted a reluctant cat back on deck. "We've gotta put Porky up for the night big guy. I'll take you ashore tomorrow."

That evening Tune-up never left Matt's side and even curled up at the end of his bunk for the night. The odd behavior was not lost on the captain.

Theodora madly paced the deck, frustrated with the cat's protective maneuver.

"What's wrong with our highness," Porky asked, as he dealt Thelma a gin hand.

"Oh, pay her no mind. She has it in for the ship's cat. Won't give the poor thing any peace."

"Why not? He's a nice cat. He doesn't use his claws when he rides on me."

"It's just her insecurities showing, dear. Now play your hand."

Porky drew. "She doesn't seem insecure to me." He leaned close to Thelma and whispered, "But she's a little scary."

"Don't let her airs fool you, dear. She's just like the rest of us."

The queen finally tired and joined the others in the engine room. "My feet are killing me." She kicked off her shoes and wiggled her toes at Porky. "I'd like a foot rub."

Porky jerked back, astonished, his card-hand all but forgotten. "You...you want me to rub...rub your feet?" He was having trouble processing this unbelievable request by the queen. His wildest dreams didn't come close.

"Of course I mean you. Now put down the cards and get busy."

Porky gave Thelma an anxious, questioning look.

Thelma laid down her hand. "Go right ahead, dear. We can play later."

The next morning Matt grabbed his laptop and rowed Tune-up ashore, but the cat didn't seem all that anxious to leave the dinghy. Along the road to the dockyard he came to a café advertised as a Wi-Fi hotspot. Its outdoor tables with green umbrellas were nearly full of folks in floppy hats, T-shirts and shorts bent over their online devices—the cruising crowd. The smell of cooked bacon blanketed the area. Matt's stomach rumbled. A chalkboard on the left side of the brick façade advertised breakfast burritos, French toast and eggs. On the right was a large corkboard covered with all manner of notices. He set his pack on an empty table and lifted Tune-up onto a chair. "You guard this stuff. I'll be right back."

He went in and placed his order then came back, cup of coffee in hand, to study the message board. He noted several crew wanted cards and briefly considered this as an option for himself, but was in no hurry to go that route. A wide range of yacht equipment, from assorted line and hardware to electronics was offered for sale or trade. He was just about to turn away when he noticed a for-sale card that read: 3meter Zodiac with a 4 hp Yamaha outboard, like new. Contact *Cher*, Falmouth. VHF16.

Matt returned to his table. "Our Frenchman's been busy," he told the cat. "What do you wanna bet there's a theft reported for that dinghy back in Redhook?"

His humongous burrito arrived, delivered by a 200 pound black lady. "Here you go skipper. You eat all that and you'll look like me," she said and let loose a peal of laughter as she hustled off.

"She ain't kiddin', big guy. There's plenty here for you."

While he ate, he checked e-mails, and just for grins, sent the colonel a note asking if he knew who Thelma was. Then, out of curiosity he Googled *stolen zodiac 4hp Yamaha*.

The eighth listing down was a link to a blog from cruisers-net.com. He clicked on it. Under theft reports was a post by the yacht *Ringer: Our white 10-foot Zodiac with a 4hp Yamaha outboard was stolen off the davits in Redhook Bay, St. Thomas, on April 03, 2012. This was a new unit and uninsured. Reward offered for its return.* Serial numbers and contact info followed.

"Well, dang, big guy, that was only six days ago and I guarantee we're the only ones who know about it." He took a screen-shot of the posting and mulled options while he shared the rest of his burrito with the cat.

Before heading back to the boat, Matt crowded up to the message board and popped the Zodiac for-sale card off the board and slipped it in his pocket. *Don't want that puppy sold and miss a chance to bust this guy.*

As he rowed back to *TR* he saw that the white Zodiac was still tied to the Frenchman's boat. He thought about going over himself for a closer look, but with *le chat* from hell along he was pretty sure René would figure things out and get the hell outta Dodge.

Back at the boat, Tune-up clung to Matt like a fly on dead fish. Now and then he'd let out a guttural yowl. Matt was mystified, but couldn't help thinking about what Shanna and Per had brought up.

Chapter 31

Matt had just finished a peanut butter and banana sandwich and was still undecided about what action to take concerning the Frenchman when he heard a powerful outboard approach.

"Ahoy, *Theodora R.*"

Matt smiled as he climbed into the cockpit. Shanna was at the helm of a slick center-console Boston Whaler with a green Bimini top. "Ahoy, yourself." He tied two fenders on the port side of *TR*.

She maneuvered the Whaler expertly alongside, handed Matt the painter, then stepped aboard and greeted the cat. She wore the same green shorts with a loose yellow T-shirt that had a profile of *Shanella* on the front.

"Nice surprise," Matt said.

"We had a lull so I thought I'd take *Shanella's* tender for a spin. What are you up to?"

"Couple of things. First, Tune-up is acting really bizarre, totally agitated on board, but quite calm ashore. And, I've got an e-mail out to the guy I bought the boat from, asking for background on Thelma."

"That could prove interesting." She scratched the cat behind its ears.

"Secondly, is a problem with your friend, René."

She arched her eyebrows. "How so?"

Matt pulled the card he'd taken off the notice board from his pocket and handed it to her.

She read it and handed it back. "What's the problem, do you want to buy it?"

"No, and the reason there is a problem is because there appears to be no problem."

Her brow knit and she tilted her head. "Huh?"

"So here's the backstory." Matt told her how Tune-up had foiled the attempted theft of his inflatable dingy back in Redhook Bay and his meeting René when he was buying hydrogen peroxide at the store because of *le chat* from hell.

Shanna shook her head. "So you think he stole that dinghy? That seems pretty thin and circumstantial, Matt. I'd say you're stretching things a bit. René's an okay guy." She grinned and asked, "You're not the jealous type are you?"

He huffed a short laugh. "That's precisely why I didn't say anything yesterday when I found out you knew him. But there's more. Come below and I'll show you."

Seated at the dinette, he fired up his computer. "On a hunch, I googled that dinghy and motor described on the card and this is what came up." He showed her the screen shot of the theft posting from six days ago.

Shanna read it in silence, then breathed out a quiet "Whoa, that changes things."

"Exactly. I'm just not sure how to proceed."

"We can go to the police."

Matted liked the "we" part. "You think they'll even care about something happening in the U.S. Virgin Islands?"

"Dad knows the constables here. With your Google search, they should be able to act."

"Able is not the same as willing, but I'm getting ahead of myself—first things first. Let's show this stuff to your dad."

They raced out of Falmouth, around the next point of land and shot through the dogleg entrance to English Harbor. The outboard echoed off the high rock walls until Shanna coasted up to *Shanella's* bow.

Bill was just sending off some visitors and came forward to lend a hand. "Well look what the tide washed up. Good to see you again, Matt."

"Hope I smell better than that," Matt said and sniffed at his armpit.

"Wait'll you hear this Dad. Remember the Frenchman we met last year, René?"

"You just missed him," Bill said, laughing. "He stopped by a half hour ago."

Shanna glanced at Matt, who asked, "He didn't try and sell you a dinghy did he?"

A look of surprise popped on Bill's face. "Odd you should say that. He mentioned he had one for sale. Wanted fifteen hundred for it. I said I'd pass the word. What's going on?"

Back in the shaded comfort of the cockpit, Matt went over the story again.

Bill gave a low whistle. "Well I'll be damned."

"I know you're friendly with the police here," Shanna said. "Do you think they'll listen?"

He stood and hung up a 'be back shortly' sign. "One way to find out—let's go."

The cop-shop was located at the far north end of the restored barracks, shaded by a large tamarind tree. The trio entered the small air-conditioned annex. Proclamations and posters of outlaws decorated the walls. There were two metal folding chairs in front of a single desk with a computer, manned by a sharply dressed, thirtyish constable in navy slacks with a red stripe down the side and a crisp white jacket. His nametag read Constable Johnson.

"Ahh, Captain Sykes, you're not leaving us so soon are you?"

"No no, I'll be here till the show's over." We have something else we need to run by you. Concerns a stolen Zodiac and outboard."

Johnson leaned forward, gesturing to the empty chairs. "Please, have a seat and tell me about it."

Bill introduced Matt and said, "Take it from the top."

And for the third time in so many hours, Matt started with Tune-up shredding the Frenchman's wrist. He ended by handing the constable the For Sale card he'd taken from the message board and showing him the Google screen-shot. Johnson booted up his computer and asked where Matt had found the posting. A few minutes later, after confirming the current date on the post, is was clear to Johnson that the thief was in his back yard.

"I'll contact my sergeant about this. He'll want to check with the police at Redhook about the Zodiac, but in the meantime, I can tell you *Cher* hasn't cleared in with our offices, which is required within twelve hours. His vessel will be detained until all this is sorted out."

Shanna stepped forward, "He has two dogs aboard. What will happen to them if he's arrested?"

Johnson hesitated, then said, "Unless this fellow doesn't cooperate with us he will likely be told to leave Antigua immediately and he and his vessel will be blacklisted throughout the Caribbean. If for any reason we detain him for any length of time, the dogs will be put down."

Matt could see Shanna wasn't all that thrilled about the possibility the dogs could be put down, but he thanked Johnson and shook his hand.

Johnson nodded. "Thank you for bringing this to our attention. We want to keep the yachting community happy."

"No problem. And if you don't mind, I'll e-mail the folks on *Ringer* and let them know where to find their dinghy."

"Please do and we'll follow it up with confirmation of our own."

After they left the constable, Matt turned to Bill. "What's your take? Think they'll just boot him out?"

"Most likely. It's the easiest and least expensive way to deal with the situation. And being blacklisted is fairly serious punishment. He's basically kicked out of the Caribbean."

"I'm more concerned about the dogs than René at this point," Shanna said.

Bill draped an arm across her shoulders. "That's another reason they'll kick him out. The police don't want to have to deal with the dogs. Makes things messy."

The whole of the dockyard had Wi-Fi, so as soon as they returned to *Shanella*, Matt fired off an e-mail to the folks on *Ringer* with the good news. He also checked his inbox and found a reply from the colonel:

Matt,

Good to hear from you and pleased to know you haven't soured on the adventure. Sometimes the dream doesn't match the reality. Mind you, can't say as I miss the actual sailing. I trust the old girl is treating you well. As for Thelma, I can't speak for the original owner since I'd never met him, but in England a Thelma is a stereotypical frumpish housewife with curlers in her hair, dressed in a housecoat and wearing fuzzy slippers. But don't let that put you off. I found this definition before I bought the boat. It convinced me to keep the name.

Thelma: *Nurturer / Caregiver: Stubborn at times and strong-willed. Likely to hurt one's feelings if unprepared for brutal honesty, but well-intentioned and loving. Loves to laugh, but because of past hurts may mask her tenderness by putting up a wall. Once you crack the shell she's a kitty cat. Thelma's have a wild side as well—get to know one.*

"Wow, listen to this e-mail I just got from the guy who sold me the boat," Matt said. He read it aloud then looked up. "Maybe I *was* too hasty in renaming the boat."

Chapter 32

"Ya' Think?" Shanna laughed and handed Matt a tall glass of iced tea. "If that bio of Queen Theodora you showed me yesterday is anything to go by, you might want to reconsider the decision."

Matt closed his laptop and took a swig of tea, giving himself time to mull it over. "Maybe, but the thought of trying to re-register from here is enough to put me off the idea."

"I might have a solution for you," Bill said. "But let's not be hasty." He winked at Shanna and they all laughed. "Come for dinner tonight and I'll show you a trick."

"Sounds great, you're on."

Just then more potential charterers arrived at the gangplank. Shanna tilted her head toward the bow. "C'mon, I'll run you home."

During the run to Falmouth they speculated on the fate of the Frenchman. Matt had leaned in close to speak over the engine noise and was tantalized by Shanna's natural scent, a mix of dark chocolate and almonds. He was tempted to take a bite. *Easy does it, Buddy, she'll be gone in a few days and you don't need any heart tweaks right now.*

She eased *Shanella's* tender up to *Theodora R*, then scanned the anchorage—all was quiet. "Sorry I can't stick around and watch the action, but I'd best get back and give Dad a hand. If it's slow tomorrow, I'll give you a hand with the sewing machine."

Matt gave her shoulder a squeeze then stepped aboard. "Whatever, it's not a huge priority. Thanks for the help. See you tonight."

She flashed him a smile and roared off.

Matt puzzled over the absence of his first mate until he heard a cranky meow come from the dinghy. Tune-up was perched on the bow, just out of range for a return leap to *TR*. Matt pulled Porky in and the cat sprang to the deck. "What the devil are you doing out there? Need another trip to shore? I thought you were content staying aboard." He went below for his binoculars, the cat

135

following him in and out of the boat. Matt shook his head. "What is with you?"

An hour after Shanna left, a navy blue police launch with two uniformed officers aboard shot into the harbor. Matt focused the binoculars on it and recognized one of them as Constable Johnson. The launch slowed as it entered the fleet of anchored yachts and wound its way toward the head of the bay. When it reached *Cher* it circled twice as fenders were flipped out on the port side. Both dogs set up a mad barking. They appeared to be tied to the mast. Matt could see René gesticulating wildly as the police launch nudged alongside and tied off. He wished he could hear the exchange. René ducked below, then reappeared and handed the police some documents.

Matt walked to the bow where he had a better view. The cat sat and leaned against his leg. He could feel the vibration of his purr all the way up his spine.

Thelma had been quietly observing the relentless pursuit of the cat by Theodora and was relieved when he'd jumped to the dinghy. The queen was so focused on her own agenda she couldn't grasp the big picture, the one where Matt woke up to the real possibility of a spirit world. Thelma could only hope the queen would continue the harassment while the captain was aboard.

The two cops were now pointing toward a dock to their left. René was shaking his head until Johnson showed him his sidearm and pointed to the dogs. René lifted his hands in surrender, moved forward and began hauling in his anchor line. As soon as the anchor was up, the launch moved toward the dock with *Cher* still tied alongside.

"Busted," Matt said softly.

Tune-up's purr turned to a growl. Matt looked down and saw his ears laid back, eye riveted on the forward hatch. "Now what? You're making me nervous Mister Mate." *Shit, I hope he's not rabid or anything. For all I know he suffers from psychotic episodes.* "Are you supposed to be medicated, big guy? Let's get you ashore for a little walk."

The cat readily followed Matt into the dinghy, but when they reached shore he refused to leave the craft. Instead, he curled up in a shady corner of the stern.

Porky, now confident that Tune-up meant him no harm, had become quite fond of the animal and cherished their brief times together. He couldn't be happier with the company.

Matt, on the other hand, was exasperated. After several attempts to coax the cat ashore he threw up his hands and stalked off toward the dock where the police had towed the Frenchman. A police vehicle was now parked there and a cop with sergeant stripes had joined the other two from the launch. Their attention had turned to the dinghy. Johnson appeared to be checking the serial numbers, then looked up and nodded to the sergeant.

Matt found a convenient bench within earshot and sat unnoticed. The police activity had attracted attention from folks on the other boats at the dock.

The sergeant handed René some papers. After studying the paper for a moment, he looked up. "But I have not stolen this dinghy. I have bought it from a man on St. John."

The sergeant said, "As you can see, the craft has been reported stolen. Do you have a receipt of sale?"

René threw his arm toward the dinghy. "But this is not new. I paid the man with Euros. I have no receipt."

The sergeant lifted his head. "I'm sorry, but without proper proof of ownership, we must confiscate it. And furthermore, because you have blatantly ignored our requirements for entry into Antigua," he nodded to the constables, "these gentleman will now escort you out of the harbor. You are no longer welcome here."

"But…But, you cannot do this. I have no supplies."

"We will see that you have water in your tanks. Guadeloupe is not far." He turned toward constable Johnson. "Secure the dinghy to our dock. Stay with him for at least one mile outside the harbor." He turned back to René. "You are lucky we haven't confiscated your vessel, condemned your dogs and locked you in jail. Your vessel will now be blacklisted throughout the Caribbean community. Don't expect any warm welcomes." With that, he spun smartly on his heel and returned to his car.

Just then, Matt spotted Tune-up trotting onto the police dock. The dogs set up a frenzied racket when the cat sat and began licking his paws. Without thinking, Matt ran down and snatched up the goofy feline and made a hasty departure. But not before René yelled after him, "I see you, Américain."

Without looking back, Matt walked rapidly back to his dinghy. "Nice fix you've got us in now Mister Mate. I hope we've seen the last of him." Tune-up was all purrs and again Matt wondered about his odd behavior. "I don't know what's gotten in to you, but you're on probation now. A boat's too small to have a whacky cat aboard."

Chapter 33

Matt was in his stateroom up forward in a futile search for a clean, unwrinkled shirt, Tune-up glued to his side. "You think I need help with this, buddy?" He lifted the feline through the forward hatch and set him on the deck. "Why don't you hang out topside until I get sorted out down here."

The queen watched the cat, a snarling grin on her face. She turned to Thelma. "I've got him on the run now. The captain is sure to put him ashore if he keeps up the shadow act."

Thelma's natural tendency was to point out the flaws in the queen's thinking, that considering his fondness for his first mate, it would take a lot more than the cat shadowing the captain's every move to doom the poor thing to exile. But she held her tongue and instead decided to let her majesty walk a plank of her own construction. "I'd say he's as skittish as a rat on a sinking ship. A bit more of your relentless torment and he's bound to jump ship on his own."

Sensing the exchange between the two spirits lounging on the foredeck, Tune-up's head swiveled from port to starboard, his good eye seeming to penetrate into their world.

After a quick sniff of the pits on an almost wrinkle-free polyester hibiscus-print shirt, Matt buttoned it up and turned to duck through the galley. But, for the first time since his voyage began he paused, reached out his hand and let his fingertips brush over the carved letters THELMA. *I believe I might owe you an apology old girl. I definitely made some assumptions and didn't give you a fair trial.*

Transfixed as she was on the cat, Theodora failed to note the actions of the captain, but Thelma missed none of it and a soft smile lit her face.

Matt ruffled the cat's ears as he stood in the dinghy ready to row ashore. "You behave yourself, Mister Mate. Keep a close eye on things while I'm gone." As he sat and pulled on the oars, Tune-up gave a mournful yowl, looked over his shoulder and hissed.

Matt cocked his head, pondering the cat. *I'd love to know what's goin' through that head of yours.*

Aboard *Shanella* Bill Sykes had fired up a rail-mounted gas grill. There were fish filets and skewered vegetables on the cockpit table. Matt could see Shanna below in the galley hacking away at something with a big knife. They both wore tan shorts and navy t-shirts with *Shanella* embroidered on the front.

Bill handed him a cold beer. "What's the news on our friend?"

Shanna's face appeared in the companionway. "Is he gone?"

Matt leaned back in the cockpit, took a long swig of brew, purposefully drawing out the moment. Finally he smiled. "Escorted out of the harbor by the police two hours ago."

"They didn't take the dogs did they," Shanna asked.

"Uh uh, took the whole kennel with him. After verifying the serial numbers, they asked him if he had a receipt for the dinghy and that sealed his fate. Topped him up with water and sent him on his way. Told him he'd be blacklisted throughout the Caribbean and not to expect any warm welcomes."

Bill slid the filets on the grill. "Good. Maybe he'll sail back to France."

Shanna gave Matt a questioning look. "How do you know what they told him? Were you there?"

"Yeah, Tune-up was acting kinda weird so I ran him ashore thinking he needed a walk. He wouldn't leave the dinghy, so I got close enough to the police dock to hear what was going on." Matt laughed. "Just as they were casting him off Tune-up walks down the dock and starts cleaning himself in front of the dogs. They set up a hell of a racket so I had to run down and haul him away. Unfortunately, René recognized the cat, and me, and let me know it. I'll have to steer clear of him in the future. It wouldn't take a genius to realize I was probably the one who busted him."

Shanna handed Bill a plate with a skinned and sectioned pineapple on it, then climbed into the cockpit and sat. She had a glass of white wine and lifted a salute. "Cheers. I doubt we'll ever see him again, considering the blacklist."

Smoke from the grill wafted across the cockpit bringing the rich aroma of grilled veggies and seared fish. Matt's stomach rumbled. "Smells great skipper. If I was considering a charter, that would clinch the deal."

Laughing, Shanna said, "He usually gets the guests to do the cooking unless they're inept."

Bill shook his spatula at her. "Now now, I'll have you know half my return guests come for my cooking."

Matt held up his beer. "I believe it."

Shanna looked over her wineglass at Matt. "So what's up with your cat?"

"Beats me. As of yesterday he won't leave my side when I'm aboard. Acts like there's someone following him around. He wasn't at all happy when I left him alone just now."

Setting her wineglass down, Shanna gave him a frank look. "I'm sure you've heard the phrase, denial is not a river in Egypt."

Matt shrugged. "And your point?"

Shanna raised her brows and looked upward.

Bill stepped into the cockpit with a plateful of food and set it on the table. Matt's mouth began to water. "I think what Shanna is getting at is there is clear evidence that something, beyond our normal perception is going on aboard your boat and you are refusing to even acknowledge the possibility."

"Thank you, Dad," Shanna said. "Well said."

Matt frowned. "You really think Tune-up is trying to tell me something?"

"From everything you've told me and from what I've seen, I'd say it was a pretty good guess." Shanna dished up a plate and handed it to him.

"After the e-mail I got from the colonel it's obvious there's a radical personality difference in the two boat names. But what you're suggesting requires me to step way outside my belief zone and accept the existence of a spirit world."

Shanna took a bite of fish then pointed her fork at Matt. "Belief is a big step, Matt." She glanced toward Bill and he dropped his gaze to the food in front of him. "I'm just saying the evidence requires serious consideration. And like I said before, cats are pretty attuned to stuff we're not really aware of."

"I'll admit I'm a fairly pragmatic, down to earth, what you see is what you get kinda guy. This stuff is hard to get my head around, but I'm listening. The logical outcome of all this is changing the boat name back to *Thelma,* and all I see there is a big headache."

Bill looked up from his plate, "Not so big. When we're finished eating I'll show you what I mean."

"Great, and my compliments to the chef. Tasty blackening rub."

Shanna smiled. "I'll take that compliment."

"I guess I'll have to rescind the threat I made to Tune-up. I told him I'd put him ashore if he kept up his weird behavior."

Picking up a wedge of pineapple, Shanna said, "You should give him a medal or better yet, a glob of catnip. He's trying real hard to communicate with you."

Matt held his hands up in surrender. "Okay, I'll give him some slack and see where it leads.

Once the dishes were cleared from the cockpit, Bill ducked below, returning a moment later with a large manila envelope. He sat and pulled out a document with ribbons attached and handed it to Matt. "This is my boat documentation."

Matt studied the official looking paper, noting the bold heading that read CERTIFICATE OF AMERICAN OWNERSHIP with an embossed seal and an attached red ribbon on the lower right hand corner along with a couple of flourishing signatures. The body of the text described *Shanella* and her owner's particulars. He handed it back to Bill. "Very impressive."

"Available from any American consulate for about seventy-five dollars. All you need is your passport and a valid bill of sale for the vessel."

Matt opened his wallet and extracted what looked like a credit card. "This my boat registration and nobody is impressed."

"My point exactly," Bill said, chuckling. So if you decide to change the boat's name you can do it wherever you find an American consulate or embassy. Keep in mind, they probably won't do it while you wait. Figure on three to five business days. Mine took four."

Matt shrugged. "Time I've got."

Shanna came from below where she'd been on galley duty. "Where do you plan to be for the hurricane season?"

"I really hadn't thought that far ahead. Where do you keep *Shanella?*"

"In years past I've kept her in Grenada," Bill said. "But I've made arrangements with a marina in Marigot Bay in St. Lucia for this season. A good friend now runs the place."

"I've studied the chart of St. Lucia," Matt said, "and it looks like there're several descent hidey holes along the west coast. My plan is to stick fairly close to protection and keep a sharp eye to the weather so I probably won't be in just one place all season. When will you be in Marigot?"

Shanna pulled out her phone and started to scroll through some data. "The last charter ends July 10th and I don't think we'll book any later than that, will we Dad?"

"No way. July is pushing it, but those folks have come down every year. Shanna helps with that group. We'll drop them in Martinique and head directly to Marigot. I usually stay with the boat all season with a couple trips stateside."

"I may catch up with you down island then. When do you leave here?"

"I have a charter flying in day after tomorrow so we'll be out of here the next day."

Shanna poured herself another glass of wine. "I fly out on the same flight those folks come in on."

She and Bill kept Matt entertained with chartering mishaps for the rest of the evening. After Matt left, Shanna turned to her dad. "I thought you would have told Matt about Mom."

Bill shrugged. "You heard him, he was having a hard time getting his head around the possibility of some kind of spirit world. I thought it might have been more than he could handle just now."

"You might be right. I'm helping him with a sail repair tomorrow if time permits, and I'll see how things are with his first mate. He may be ready for another eye-opener by then."

Bill laughed. "Good luck with that."

As Matt rowed up to *TR* he could make out a dinghy tied to the stern. *What the hell is this all about?* When he got closer he recognized Per's little skiff and rowed along side, shipped his oars and grabbed the rail. He didn't see Per or the cat anywhere and a steady stream of water flowed from the bilge exhaust. "Hey, Per," he called, and heard a muffled reply from below. The Dane's head appeared above the companionway hatch and Tune-up leapt onto the deck. "What's goin' on?"

Per stepped into the cockpit wiping his hands on a rag. "Your boat was sinking, but I think I have the problem sorted."

Matt climbed aboard and gave the cat a pat. "Sinking?" *This oughtta be good.*

"One hour ago your cat started raising a ruckus. I thought he might be injured so I come over to have a look. The cat looks fine and then I see the water pumping out. I go below and hear water running in the stern. I open the engine hatch and know right away it is the stuffing box. I come back with a torch and spanner and tightened her up. Just a slow drip now, but still plenty of water in the bilge."

Matt picked up the cat and ruffled his head. "Looks like you earned your keep again, Mister Mate." His thunderous purr made Per laugh.

"Thanks for coming to the rescue. I installed the float switch for the bilge pump after my last near disaster. I hope this doesn't become a regular routine."

"My grandfather told me the key to a successful voyage is keep the water out."

"He got that right. Can I pour you a nightcap? You've earned it."

"Why not?"

Matt brought up the rum and filled two tumblers and lifted a toast. "Cheers, my friend. Hope I can return the favor someday."

"If I live long enough you might get your chance." Per tossed back the rum.

Matt told Per about the description of Thelma the colonel had sent. "I think I see the conflict." He and Per both howled at that.

The queen paced the foredeck, her face a dark frown. She gnawed the knuckle of her right index finger, the balled fist of her left hand pounding a slow rhythm on her thigh. Her latest attempt to be rid of the damn cat had totally backfired and now there'd be no convincing the captain he'd be better off without the beast.

Thelma huddled in the engine room rubbing her red-rimmed weepy eyes. She'd never been struck before and the flash of the queen's hand across her cheek still smarted. It wasn't her nature to meddle, but her highness had gone too far.

Poor Tune-up tried to escape the queen's torments by crawling into the bilge through the access in the chart room. When she couldn't budge the cat, Theodora decided to flush him out by flooding the bilge. Thelma caught her yanking at the greased cord in the stuffing box, but all the pleading in the world failed to dissuade her manic behavior. In desperation, Thelma grabbed the queen's wrists to stop the craziness. Theodora spun from her grasp and lashed out with the palm of her hand. Thelma fell back in utter immobilized shock.

The queen returned to her mischief and before Thelma recovered, water gushed around the propshaft through the damaged seal. It was now impossible to repack the stuffing box without tightening the large bolts on either side, a task neither spirit was up to. If the cat hadn't raised the alarm the water flow would have overwhelmed the bilge pump and sent them all to the bottom.

The tolerant accord between spirits shattered in that brief act of violence. Thelma felt rudderless. Her only experience with violent human behavior was with her first owner, but that had been directed at him, not her. How could she continue to share the confines of her hull with the queen's suicidal and unpredictable behavior. For now, she would keep her distance and hope Theodora would hang herself from her own yardarm.

Hearing Matt speak of his communication with the colonel gave her heart, but she knew in the deepest reaches of her keel that there were serious headwinds in the offing.

By the time Per rowed into the night, the bilge had been pumped dry. Thankfully the water hadn't reached the cabin sole and flooded any of his food stores again. Matt opened the engine hatch and examined the stuffing box with a powerful flashlight. He hadn't run the engine in two days. For the life of him he couldn't figure out how the seal had failed.

Chapter 34

Matt had just cleared another jammed bobbin on the sewing machine when he heard Shanna call "Ahoy, Theodora." *Ahhh, my prayers have been answered.*

He secured the tender and she hopped aboard wearing navy shorts with a pink bikini top. She glistened with sunscreen. "We were slammed this morning, but the siesta hours gave me a needed break."

"Your timing is impeccable. I was just about to give the sewing machine the float test."

"I know it well. My dad's had numerous pieces of equipment fail that test. Funny how that stuff never seems to float. So how are things otherwise?"

Matt laughed and told her of the scene he'd returned to the previous night.

Tune-up had come to greet her and sat purring at her feet. She knelt down and gave him a hearty pat. "You're an amazing cat. I hope your captain doubles your rum ration." She stood and looked over the top of her sunglasses at Matt. "I hope you're paying attention here Skipper. How's he been behaving this morning?"

"Totally cool. Been sleeping in his usual place under the dodger since breakfast."

"At the risk of belaboring my point, it seems he's reached some sort of accord with whatever had him in a fuss."

Thelma listened to the exchange with little satisfaction. Although the queen had given up her pursuit of the cat, she was now Thelma's problem. Perched as she was in the spreaders, Theodora's gloom seemed to enshroud the entire anchorage like the approaching tendrils of a major hurricane. There would be no rest with the queen in that state. One moment of slack vigilance could be the end of this cruise. Not a word had passed between them since last night.

And that dear boy, Porky. He'd come aboard expecting a hand of cards and instead found her weeping in the engine room. What could she say without setting the boy against the queen. She'd held her tongue, but could see the confusion in his face. "I'll be fine lad, just a touch of the gout." That's what she'd told him, knowing all along he wasn't convinced. The queen only added to his confusion by ignoring him completely. The sweet lad had looked at them both, scratched his head and returned to his dinghy.

Within minutes of sitting at the machine, Shanna had the bobbin tension adjusted and a clean stitch through two layers of heavy sailcloth. "You crank and I'll guide the sail."

Matt paused after a moment of hard cranking, "Wow, don't think I'd be able to do this on my own without a motor."

"Well, don't stop now. We've got thirty feet of stitching ahead of us."

"Aye aye, Sir."

"I'm only this bossy when I'd rather be doing something else."

"Wouldn't we all. What did you have in mind?"

"I have a story to tell you."

"Really? About what?"

"My mom."

"Of the almond eyes."

"That's the one, but let's finish this first."

"I'm crankin."

Less than an hour later the sail was folded and put away, good as new. Matt whipped up a couple of toasted cheese sandwiches and popped open two beers. They settled in the cockpit, ready for story time.

Shanna rolled the cool beer bottle across her forehead then took a long drink. "Are you familiar with the term, astral travel?"

Matt smiled; he could guess where this was going. "I've heard the term, but I can't say I'm familiar with it."

She noticed the smile. "Don't laugh until you hear the story."

He sat back. "Fair enough."

"My mom was an astral traveler. Several times a year she'd go into a deep sleep and, according to her, her spirit would leave her body and travel to Japan to visit her family. The first time my dad witnessed it, her breathing was so slow and shallow he thought she had died. He even called 911, but she woke up before the paramedics arrived. Dad, ever the skeptic had my mom describe one of her trips, then called her sister in Japan to see if the events matched, and sure enough they'd all been at a family picnic just as mom had described."

"Wow, Did she go anyplace besides Japan?" His eyes were locked on hers.

"Not that I know of. It was just her way of staying in touch. I've never had the experience, but that doesn't mean I don't believe it happens."

"How did she learn to do it?"

"She came to it naturally when she was about my age. I researched it and even tried some of the how-to techniques out there, so I'm hoping it occurs naturally like it did for her. That could happen at any time."

"So what you're saying to me is there's probably stuff going on around us that we are unaware of and we should keep an open mind."

She reached over and gave his leg a squeeze just above the knee. "Sharp boy."

"Sounds like your mom had a real desire for the familial connection. Maybe the level of desire triggers the ability."

"Good point, and one I've batted around myself. One can only hope."

In the silence that followed, Matt picked at the wet label on his beer bottle, then looked up. "Soooo, you're off tomorrow."

"I am, and not without regret," she said. A wry smile softened her features. "I've enjoyed getting to know you and wish we had more time. I tried to get my flight out changed, but with charter week it was impossible. Hopefully we'll cross paths again in July. I'm already looking forward to it."

"I'm on the same page. And you can count on seeing me in St. Lucia. I've got your e-mail, so let's keep in touch."

She looked at her watch and stood. "I told dad I'd be back by two. We're entertaining again tonight so this is goodbye for now."

Before she stepped aboard *Shanella's* tender she leaned into Matt and gave him a kiss that was more than a peck goodbye and hinted of promise. He hugged her tight, savored the scent of chocolate and almonds then watched until she disappeared out of the harbor.

The queen, delighted with Shanna's departure, decided to use her absence to her advantage. Since the cat was here to stay, harmony aboard would be the goal, a complete reversal of earlier tactics. She regretted slapping Thelma, but only because it made shipboard harmony a bit of a reach. Ignoring the cat would be easy. The hard part would be coming up with a convincing apology for Thelma.

Thelma, submerged in a tropical depression caused by the queen's assault and the girl's departure, felt as though she'd been run hard aground. It didn't help that Matt, taking action to get his mind off Shanna, took off on an island tour and left the first mate in charge. His parting words were, "Don't wait up." Who knew when Porky would be back to help cheer her up? Now she was stuck here with the queen.

From a mere slit in his good eye, Tune-up watched Theodora alight on the foredeck. Curled beneath the spray dodger, he tracked her every move, relaxing slightly when she gave him a wide berth as she warily made her way to the engine room in the stern.

Thelma had drifted into a fitful sleep disturbed by images of brutal hand-to-hand combat and sinking ships. She felt a slight prod to her shoulder and started awake. The queen's face filled her vision. She let out a piercing shriek and leapt to the cockpit. "Keep your distance you, you, royal menace!" She shook an admonishing finger at Theodora while backing away.

Theodora raised her hands in a placating gesture. "I'm Sorry, Thelma. I'm sorry. Please don't be afraid. I didn't mean to hit you. It was, it was…" She hung her head and stifled a sob, then looked up, her face a portrait of sorrow. "It was a like a conditioned response. I didn't have an easy childhood. Daily beatings were a part of my life. So I learned to strike back. Please believe me, it was just a survival thing. A pathetic excuse, but it's all I have. Can we start over?"

Thelma took a couple of tentative steps forward and braced her hands on her hips. "You have an odd sense of survival, Missy. You do your best to sink us then attack me for trying to save us."

The queen hung her head, not an easy thing for a monarch to do. "It was stupid, I know. I don't know what I was thinking. It was all about that damn cat."

Mention of the cat in a bad light made Thelma frown. "That damn cat, as you so unkindly put it, kept us from a watery grave and I'll not hear another slanderous remark about our first mate from the likes of you."

Oops, bad move there, sister. "You're right. I'm still not quite thinking straight. And I promise you, from this day forward, I'll hold our first mate in the highest regard."

As much as Thelma wanted to believe the queen, especially the part about her childhood abuse, there was something that smelled like the hold of a fish scow on a hot day about it. Skullduggery such as this didn't fit with Thelma's view of a leisurely lifestyle and she needed some time to digest her majesty's behavior. "I'm willing to forgive the slap, but the whole episode has fouled my rigging and I need room to maneuver before we can resume our past course."

Theodora gave a sage nod. "I understand. I'll give you all the space you need. Just so you know, I want to put this all behind us."

Retying the line around her robe with a rolling half hitch, Thelma snugged it up tight and patted down her curlers. "A truce it will be, Missy, but I'll not have you try and scuttle the ship again."

"You have my word," *And whatever else it takes to kiss your bum.*

Chapter 35

As the sun's first rays broke the horizon, Matt dragged himself aboard. It had been a long and enjoyable night with live, steel band music at Shirley Heights til 2 a.m. followed by consecutive parties on and off the land. He was pleasantly surprised to be welcomed home by Tune-up's coarse purr. He'd half dreaded this moment, wondering what new disasters awaited his return.

He lifted the cat to his shoulder and scanned the anchorage. "Looks like all is well with the world, Mister Mate. Let's hope it stays that way for the next few hours while I'm in recovery." He set the cat down, toured the deck, then went below and checked the bilge. *Wonderful, no surprises.*

Thelma gave a sigh of relief, the night having passed without royal interference. She took it as a good sign, but it was way to early set a course based on the queen's promises.

At the crack of noon, Matt brewed himself a mug of tar-black java to blast the fuzz from his brain. During the course of the night he'd come to terms with his single-hander status. Today he'd begin the necessary modifications to TR's rigging that would make the act of sailing far easier. As he set about gathering the needed line and hardware, he noticed Tune-up was no longer under foot and was back to snoozing under the spray dodger. Whatever had gotten under the first mate's skin seemed to have run its course.

Thelma kept a critical eye on her captain as he laid out more and more line along the deck, measuring tape in hand. She knew what he was planning and wanted to make sure he got it right. She gave a jump when Theodora spoke from just behind her. "This is looking like a rats nest to me."

"You're not far off, Missy. A spider's web is more like it. The captain is rigging lazy jacks to keep our mainsail under control. If he goes about it right, our sail will pile neatly atop the boom when he lets loose the halyard. Once it's all in place we'll hear a new tune when the wind whistles through the lot of it."

The queen gave her mirror the once over. "Why am I starting to feel like a serving wench wearing a hairnet. This can't possibly compliment our stainless steel."

Thelma arched one eyebrow and looked back at Theodora. "Would you rather we lose our captain overboard?"

"Of course not."

"Well, then keep in mind it's a safety issue, one used by most practical sailors. While it does add clutter aloft, if the knot-work is done with care it lends a certain nautical flair to our rig."

Theodora's concept of nautical flair bore no resemblance to Thelma's, but she held her tongue in her quest for shipboard harmony. "I suppose I'll get used to it. I see our neighbor *Brindle* has what you describe and it doesn't detract from her looks all that much."

Thelma smiled to herself, wondering how much effort it took for the queen to be so compromising. Maybe with enough practice it would become habit.

Late the following day, Matt's handiwork indeed looked as though a giant spider had spun a web in the rigging. Close to four-hundred feet of three-eights inch line hung on and about the mainsail all in an effort to help tame the three-hundred and fifty square feet of canvas.

Thelma was pleased with her captain's rope-work and pointed out the finer points to the queen. "The whipped ends and rolling hitches should meet with your grace's approval. The man who commissioned our hull would even be impressed and he was not an easy man to please when it came to seamanship."

"I'm not blind, Thelma. The captain's handiwork has not escaped my eye, but you have to admit that from more than thirty feet who would know?"

"Why in the world would I care? I know, and that allows me to carry our rig with pride."

"Where I come from it's how the rest of the world perceives me that matters."

Thelma gave the queen a pitiful look. "I feel sorry for you. In my world if the captain respects the traditions of sailing craft, that is all I need to keep me on an even keel. So far I've been fortunate with my captains."

The fact that someone actually felt sorry for her was totally new to Theodora. Envious, jealous, covetous, desirous, begrudging, bitter, yes, but sorry? What was that all about?

Matt had just popped a beer to celebrate a project well done when he heard the approach of a small outboard engine. He climbed to the cockpit just as a sunbaked, middle-aged couple dressed in the yachties ubiquitous gear came along side. He recognized the dinghy as the one rescued from the Frenchman.

He took the dinghy's painter and invited them aboard. "Glad to see you got it back."

The woman spoke. "You can't imagine our surprise when we got your e-mail. Set sail straight away and arrived last night."

The man extended his hand. "I'm Gene, and this is my wife Helen, off *Ringer.*"

They shook hands. "Matt, a pleasure." He held up his beer. "Can I offer you one?"

Gene glanced at his wife. "Yes, please."

Tune-up hopped out from under the dodger and gave them a welcoming purr as loud as their outboard, but not as smooth.

"Who's this big fella?" Gene reached down to give him a pat.

"That would be my first mate, Tune-up. He figures prominently in the story I have for you."

Once settled in the cockpit, Matt gave them a rundown on how he suspected the dinghy had been stolen and notifying the police. "The whole series of events put me in a unique position." Matt chose not to burden them with the fact that René had recognized him and held him responsible for his blacklisting.

Helen shook her head in wonder. "What are the odds? Too bad we weren't in a casino"

Reaching into his pocket, Gene withdrew an envelope. "Speaking of which, we'd posted a five–hundred dollar reward in Red Hook for the return of our dinghy. So this is yours."

Matt waved off the offer. "Look Gene, if I needed it I'd take it. Do me a favor and help out someone down the line who could really use it."

Helen leaned forward, grabbed Matt's left hand and with the other, jerked the envelope from Gene and slapped it into Matt's palm. "Don't be silly. We won't take no for an answer and you can dispose of it as you see fit."

"But…"

She held up one hand. "End of discussion. And please come to dinner on *Ringer* tomorrow. Gene's a gourmet chef. You won't regret it."

Matt caved to the onslaught and accepted all offers.

Gene pointed out the yellow hull of *Ringer* and they stood to leave. "Oh, I wanted to say you have a lovely vessel here, a really fine example of traditional craftsmanship. I can see you take care with her upkeep."

"Labor of love."

Thelma nudged the queen. "See what I mean, Missy."

After they'd left, he tucked the envelope of money in the hidey-hole with the rest of his funds, trying to think of how best to spread the wealth. He gave up after a couple of hours and decided the answer would present itself at the right time.

The next morning, Matt went for another breakfast burrito at the Internet café. He'd composed an e-mail to Shanna describing his boat upgrades and the visit from the folks off *Ringer*. When he logged on he was pleasantly surprised to find a note from her.

Matt,

Welcomed home by heavy rain and cold temps. Should of hung around a bit longer. Shoulda-woulda-coulda. What's a girl to do? Missing the Carib fiercely and getting to know you and *Theodora* (or should I say *Thelma*?). Big art show coming up, a real moneymaker for me. Have already booked tickets for my return in July. Hope to see you.

A soggy farewell, Shanna

After reading Shanna's e-mail, Matt made a few revisions to his own, adding a line about missing her as well and made a commitment to July. He'd originally had something to that effect, but decided it might sound a little too pushy and had reduced things to a news bulletin. He was grateful to her for opening the door so he could let a little emotion flow, knowing it wasn't one-way.

Chapter 36

Ten days of island time drifted by and Thelma finally relaxed into the gentle swell always present in the anchorage. The queen's attack became a dull, disquieting memory. Her captain continued with his upgrades and reintroduced the sliding forestay the colonel had engineered. The device would keep him from having to go out on her bowsprit to change sails—always dicey, if alone. Of course Theodora had had her sails aback over the additional rigging aloft, but conceded that the captain not having to leave the safety of the deck outweighed her vain need for an unencumbered rig.

And Theodora, for her part, had kept clear of the cat. Also, the few times Porky had had the opportunity to join them she kept a civil tongue and was even a gracious loser at gin rummy. Could it be that her highness had really come about onto a favorable tack? Thelma kept her skepticism on short scope, not wanting to rock the boat. Even Porky kept a wary eye on the queen, unaccustomed as he was to her geniality. Of course, all the queen had to do was wiggle her toes at the poor boy and he was malleable as the tar in her deck seams.

With the end of charter week in Antiqua the anchorage had slowly emptied out. Per had set sail for the Azores and the Med for the summer season. *Ringer* had left for the Dutch Antilles and *TR's* closest neighbor was a hundred yards off. Matt stood on the helmsman's seat watching the sunset, one arm draped over the boom and a cool beer in his other hand. Tune-up perched on the mainsail cover next to him disturbing the peace. "Whadda ya' think Mister Mate? Ready for a new adventure? The forecast is for brisk easterlies for the next week and it's time to test all the changes I've made." Matt gently cuffed the big cat's ear. "Let's run down to Guadeloupe tomorrow and see how the French do things." Matt had kept a close eye on the cat and seen none of the odd behavior exhibited when they'd first arrived. In fact, since their encounter with the Frenchman, Tune-up hadn't been ashore and seemed entirely content to hang out on the boat. Matt was delighted with the mate's preference for staying aboard. From all he'd read, traveling around the world with an animal could be a real hassle in some countries if that animal needed time ashore.

Early the next morning Matt motored to the transient dock, took on fresh water, made a quick trip to the store for provisions and sent an e-mail to friends and family with his plans. His correspondence with Shanna had progressed to both of them signing off with x's and o's.

Deshaies plotted out sixty miles south of Falmouth. It was the closest place with a decent anchorage on the northwest corner of Guadeloupe. *TR* surged out of the harbor mouth at 9 a.m. with a single reef in her main, staysail and working jib set to the twenty-knot easterly breeze. The GPS had her pegged at a consistent six and a half knots. Without voicing his thoughts Matt figured he'd be there well before dark. Once he engaged Fred, which had the mechanical strength to handle the stiff wind abeam, he was free to leave the wheel and experiment with sail adjustments to best balance the helm.

Thelma stood on the forward hatch, arms thrust wide. "What a glorious sail... Oh how I've missed this."

Theodora came up behind her, hands cupped around her mouth. "You were right about our rigging playing a different tune. I can barely hear myself think."

Thelma gave a hearty laugh. "It's a gift, Missy. Some say there lies the origin of every sea chantey sung."

The queen forced herself to turn away before she gave voice to her thoughts. *A gift my ass! I'll take my court musicians over this any day. The old biddy must be half deaf. Sounds like howling banshees to me.*

Halfway along, the seas had built to a solid eight feet with frothy tops. Matt let out a piercing whooooop! when green water churned over the port rail. Tune-up leapt from his perch under the dodger to safety below. Thelma was on the verge of admonishing the captain for not taking in another reef when he eased the mainsheet, ran forward and released the halyard. A quick jerk brought the main down and in less than a minute he winched in the second reef point and raised it back up. Thelma nodded with satisfaction. *The boy has what it takes.*

The brief spell without the mainsail had maxed out Fred's ability to steer a true course and *TR* veered off downwind. But once balance returned she was soon back on a southerly heading, still cranking out a good six knots. Matt sensed the tension ease from the rig as *TR* rolled smoothly with the swells. The dark lump in the distance soon coalesced into the mountains on Guadeloupe's northwest shore.

As they closed with the coastline a sudden shriek of wind in the rigging rolled *TR* on her beam ends, her spreaders nearly touching the sea. He lurched for the wheel as the deck tilted close to vertical. The crash of shifting stores and a yowl from the mate came from below. Matt held tight with one hand and with the other released the jib-sheet from its winch. The effect was instantaneous. *TR* rolled to an even keel. The jib flailed in the wind sounding like an aerial gunfight.

Matt, busy forward, saw the next downdraft hit the water, blasting salt spray fifty feet in the air. He ran aft to let loose the mainsheet, but it was already free from the cleat. For a nanosecond he wondered when he'd done that. The bullet of wind hit. The boom swung wide and the mainsail dumped its wind. *TR* merely shuddered and remained upright.

The first downdraft had even caught Thelma off guard, but she knew more would come. The captain's quick action kept them from serious damage and his attention was now focused on subduing the jib. She saw the queen with a death-grip on the spreaders and knew there would be no help from that quarter. Fortunately, Matt had lashed Porky, fully inflated, to the cabin top. He sat atop the lashings, bewildered.

Thelma grabbed the lad's hand. "All hands big fella, we have work to do." She led him to the mainsheet cleat. "Help me get this loose. I can't manage on my own."

They tugged with all their worldly powers and, once the tailing end eased its grip, it was a simple matter to lift the loop off the cleat.

"We did it, Thelma, we did it." Porky was so pleased he almost smothered her with a hug.

"That we did, my boy," came her muffled reply. *Lucky for us you were at hand. With my powers at half throttle I'm all but useless in a crisis.* She glanced upward at Theodora still clutched to her perch. *No thanks to you.*

The new lazy-jacks worked like the web it resembled to contain the billowing main. It gave Matt the time he needed to drop both headsails, secure them to the rails and start the engine. There was no avoiding further downdrafts, but without sails they had no bite.

Tune-up's head appeared in the companionway. "We lucked out that time, Mister Mate. That could have been an expensive lesson. How are things below? The cat looked back over his shoulder then silently curled up under the dodger. "That bad, huh?"

TR's anchor chain rattled out at 6 p.m. There were only five other boats anchored in the bay at Deshaies. Matt was relieved to note *Cher* wasn't among them. A marina on the south side looked near full, but he didn't peg René for a marina type guy.

A can of vegetable beef soup and Ramen noodles made for a late dinner after Matt finished restoring order from the chaos below. Unless nailed down it had moved or been entirely displaced and Matt came to the sad conclusion that nothing had been nailed down.

Steep and green is how Matt classified the terrain surrounding the bay. The harbor was rimmed with a hodgepodge of colorful structures with no real definition between private residences and commercial buildings. Matt rowed to the marina where he found customs and immigration in what looked to him like a fast food cart at the marina entrance, near the fuel dock. They signed his name, passport number and vessel name into an oversized logbook, stamped the passport and bid him a good day. In good spirits he wandered off to explore the town. Just outside the marina entrance was a combination wine and shoe store, his first hint that the French had a different sense of priorities.

Chapter 37

Thelma was furious with the queen. She could almost forgive her for the paralytic fright that possessed her during the knockdown. After all, it was her first and Thelma could still recall her own shameful reaction the first time her original owner allowed her to broach in a big sea, nearly capsizing with breaking waves abeam. She'd cried for hours. But this hussy had the affront to act as though her behavior was of no consequence. Motoring into the harbor the previous night, Thelma had tried to point out to the queen that due to their diminished powers all hands were needed in a crisis. Theodora had looked her straight in the eye and said, "Whatever do you mean? I did my bit and look at us, not a speck of damage."

The brazen denial of her actions had left Thelma speechless. *Oh, Missy, I believe you've slipped your mooring.* This was another side of the queen she hadn't yet seen, and a dark side it was.

When Matt returned to the boat bearing a selection of French wines, two baguettes and a block of smelly cheese, he was oblivious to the tension aboard. Tune-up was pacing the deck and Matt wrote it off to the ship-bound first mate needing exercise. Matt had actually been thinking all morning about how well things aboard had gone lately. And after surviving yesterday's mayhem unscathed, he considered the cruising side of things on a definite upswing. He'd gone so far as mentally tabling, for the time being, the idea of renaming his boat.

Below, after indulging in the gastronomical delights of another culture, Matt spread a chart of the Windward Islands on the table. With a pencil he drew a small circle around Marigot Bay in St. Lucia. There was no question that he would be there when *Shanella* arrived after their last charter. Allowing himself the next two months to get there, he backtracked up the island chain, past Martinique and Dominica to his present position at the north end of Guadeloupe, getting some idea of the time and distances involved. Although the distance only computed to a few hundred miles, there was a lot of interesting ground to cover on the three intervening islands. And now that he'd gotten his first glimpse of a French island, he was in no hurry to leave its shores. He plotted out the next day's sail and pulled Porky aboard for a morning departure.

Thelma did her best to remain civil to the queen when Porky insisted on another night of cards. Theodora carried on as though all was well, but from behind his fanned-out hand, Porky's eyes strayed frequently to Thelma and she knew he sensed her unease.

Ever since her captain's lady friend had departed the tide of change had run out, taking with it any sense of urgency regarding Theodora and how the name affected the well-being of the vessel. The queen had been on the brink of her own demise when she unfortunately came to her senses and ceased her meddling. Thelma was in foreign waters, fathoming out how to turn that tide.

The steep and green theme held for the entire leeward side of Guadeloupe, with sporadic settlements clustered along the coastal road. Matt had chosen to motor along close in for the view. To pick up a clean wind for sailing, he'd have to be several miles out and miss out on any interesting detail. The radio forecast promised moderate easterlies for next few days, so Matt left *TR* double anchored in the open roadstead at Basse-Terre and hopped a small tour bus to the top of the sleeping Soufriere volcano. The four-hour ride up a winding unimproved road kept him enthralled as they rose through rain forests and into tall pines until topping out on a sulfur-infused moonscape, nearly a mile high. He caught occasional glimpses of *TR* along the way, a mere sliver of white on the ocean below.

Theodora stood at the end of her bowsprit, arms akimbo, face in a deep frown as she watched a rust-streaked interisland freighter disgorge its cargo. "Why here? No harbor, nobody but us around for miles, just this ugly commercial wharf. What's the point?"

Thelma had initially been concerned about the open roadstead, but relaxed when the captain set a second anchor. She'd felt them both dig deep into a soft bottom. "Get used to it, Missy. Our captain is an explorer and I think we'll find ourselves in some rather out-of-the-way places. Admirers will be rare as barnacles on an albatross."

Like a prophecy, that is how the next six weeks unfolded. With the official start of hurricane season on June 1st, charter boats and cruising boats alike seemed to vanish. Early on, Matt had spotted *Shanella* when he'd been poking around the Saints, a group of small islands south of Guadeloupe. He'd exchanged a quick word with Bill who looked like he had his hands full with two couples aboard. Matt had left him with the promise to meet again in Marigot.

Bill had mentioned that from his correspondence with Shanna it seemed Matt had made quite an impression on his daughter. That bit of news made him eager for the coming reunion, but had the frustrating effect of drastically slowing time.

Luckily, there had been no sightings of *Cher* anywhere around Guadeloupe. Matt began to believe René had chosen to leave Caribbean waters.

After a short overnight sail to the town of Portsmouth, on the north end of Dominica, Matt again set two anchors in the wide-open bay. There was only one other cruising sailboat in the anchorage and he learned from them that the island was well worth exploring. Armed with current intel, Matt advised his first mate that he'd be gone for a day or two. "Keep a sharp lookout and repel all boarders, Mister Mate." It was the first time Matt had decided to leave *TR* on her own overnight. He set out the cat's food under the dodger, locked the hatches and rowed ashore. He was nervous about leaving the boat unattended, but after considerable thought decided if he couldn't leave the boat on her own as needed, he'd miss out on a lot of travel experiences, especially when cruising continental ports of call.

Though satisfied with the two anchors in place, Thelma felt uneasy knowing the queen would most likely be of little help in an emergency. Porky went ashore with the captain and the mate could hardly be expected to lend a hand other than to sound the alarm. Her inherent sense of the weather told her there was nothing in the offing at present and that she could trust her captain's decision.

Theodora had grown quite bored with the solo cruising gig. It seemed she had little to live for without public adulation. There was only so much a woman could do for herself when it was all for naught.

On the third day Thelma began to worry about the captain. She'd heard him tell the mate a day or two and here the sun was about to set and tomorrow would make four. Even the mate seemed pensive, pacing the deck without the queen's provocation. As for her majesty, she'd actually gotten a little slothful, her fingers and toes showing chips in the polish, hair gone awry, white robes showing the odd smudge.

Just before dark, Thelma had made a trip to the top of her mast for a last look-see. She returned to the deck muttering. "I'm not liking this one bit. The mate's almost out of food and there're mare's tails in the sky. A shift in the weather is sure to come."

With the morning sun came a low swell working its way into the bay. "You feel that, Missy? Our wind's clocking to the south. If it keeps up and swings to the west we could find ourselves on the beach."

From her usual perch on the spreaders Theodora called down. "Get used to it, Missy, our captain's an explorer."

The taunt hit home and Thelma resumed her vigil of the shoreline. It wasn't that she questioned her captain's judgment, but she worried for his safety ashore.

By noon the swell had *TR* rolling through forty degrees and things were beginning to rattle around down below. An hour later she finally spotted Matt launching the dinghy from shore. Awash with relief she cried out her joy. Tune-up's ears perked up and his tail twitched as he leapt to the rail for a look-see, his engine sputtering at full throttle. The queen was silent, but a smile had erased her ever-present frown.

Having gotten drenched launching the dinghy in the growing onshore swell, Matt wasted no time getting under way. He hastily stowed his backpack, fresh produce and two hand-woven baskets he'd picked up on his island prowl. Amazing landscapes, waterfalls, rain forests and various artisans had demanded the extra time ashore and he didn't regret it for a minute. After a cursory inspection and finding nothing amiss, he complimented his first mate on a job well done, apologized for the delay and promised to leave more food out the next time he left him in charge.

Since he'd seen plenty of Dominica and there were no protected anchorages on this side of the island, he laid a course direct for Martinique. With the moderate breeze holding steady in the southeast, Matt lashed Porky to the cabin top, retrieved the anchors and headed south by southwest. And all went well until he sailed out of the island's wind shadow.

Chapter 38

Despite the precaution of a double-reefed main and single headsail, the passage between the two high islands gave him a thrashing. The funneled wind increased to thirty knots, turning the seas into a wild herd of white horses. Busting through ten-foot standing waves caused by wind against current, TR's decks were frequently awash in green water. Conditions were too rough for Fred to handle, so Matt spent the entire day at the helm, knee deep in water that never had the chance to drain from the cockpit.

As soon as TR began bucking in the seas, the queen again clung to the spreaders with her head buried in her arms. Thelma knew her call for all hands would be ignored. As yet there was nothing amiss, but in these conditions that could change with the snap of a shackle. She consoled herself with the knowledge that Porky could be counted on in a pinch, even though he seemed preoccupied with the wild ride.

The float switch for the bilge pump allowed for a generous amount of water to accumulate before turning on the pump. In the turbulent seas, bilge water began sloshing onto some of Matt's canned goods stored low in the lockers. After an hour of this the labels came loose and peeled from the cans and jars.

Thelma felt more than heard the strain of her bilge pump. A quick peek was all she needed to see the problem. She tugged on Porky's hand. "C'mon, me lad, we've got work ahead of us." She led him to the bilge and pointed out the soggy paper labels clogging the pump's intake screen. "Between the two of us we can pull the paper clear." She patted a spot on the floor of the chart room. "Here's where we'll stow the mess so they don't get loose in the bilge again."

They were kept busy for nearly two hours, as each small handful took all their combined strength to overcome the suction of the pump. Plus, there were constantly more labels making their way into the bilge. When finally the bilge was clear of debris, a wad of paper the size of a softball lay mounded on the floor of the chart room.

Thelma tweaked Porky's cheek. "You're a champ, my boy. I hope our captain never takes to towing you astern." She gestured upward with her thumb. "You-know-who isn't fit for this life. It's up to us to keep a weather eye out."

Porky wiped his hands on his madras shorts. "You can count on me, Thelma. But I don't know much about sailboats, so you'll have to tell me what to do."

Within the hour, conditions eased as TR entered the wind shadow of Martinique. Matt turned the helm over to Fred. He ducked below to check the British Admiralty Chart of Martinique for the notations of good anchorages entered by the colonel when he'd cruised the area. When he sat down his foot squished into something on the floor. He jerked his leg up, banging his knee on the underside of the chart table. Peering down he saw the wad of soggy paper Thelma and Porky had stashed on the floor. He reached down and scooped it up. *What the hell is this? And how did it get here?* He pulled the glob apart and immediately saw what it was. A quick look in the stores locker confirmed his observation. The shiny unlabeled cans promised a plethora of surprise meals. Unfortunately, it did nothing to solve the riddle as to how the wad ended up on the floor of the chart room.

During the passage the wind had backed into the east again, flattening the seas on the steep and green lee side of Martinique. Matt dropped anchor as soon as he picked up a wi-fi connection just off the beach at Saint Pierre. He fixed himself a bowl of popcorn and washed it down with two beers while he checked his e-mail.

In a note from Shanna, she asked if he'd seen that the first tropical storm of the season had formed west of the Cape Verde Islands. Matt brought up the South Atlantic weather satellite and there was the orange and red blob moving east at ten miles per hour. The projected path covered all the Windward Islands except Grenada. Tune-up sat beside Matt, his good eye focused intently on the screen. "Could be trouble, Mister Mate. We'll have to watch this one closely. Got a couple of weeks yet, so no worries."

Knowing what she did of the queen's recent behavior, Thelma didn't agree. The hussy was all brassy talk and no action. She couldn't imagine Theodora's reaction if it really came on to blow, but she could guarantee there'd be no help from that quarter.

Gone was the queen's disheveled state, her mirror was back and she was groomed as if to meet foreign dignitaries as they motored into the harbor at Fort de France. "Finally, someplace that matters. Time to shine, Thelma. This is how I'm meant to live."

Thelma gave a resigned sigh. "I know, I know, quietly at anchor among many admirers."

Matt happily signed the visitors' log and had his passport stamped at the customs and immigration kiosk. Rowing ashore he'd scanned the fifty-some boats at anchor, but didn't see *Cher* among them and the two dogs would be hard to miss. Caribbean island cities didn't get much bigger than this one and if someone wanted to lay low, it would be ideal.

Shortly after Matt rowed off, Theodora noticed one of her admirers in a small skiff coming by for a closer look. She preened on the foredeck, feeling resplendent. Looking toward her stern, she saw that Thelma was down for a nap. The skiff came alongside and for a moment the queen thought he meant to board or hail the captain. And oddly enough he didn't even give her so much as a look. Instead the tall, skimpily clad fellow reached into a bucket at his feet, pulled out a gray looking mass and tossed it on her deck.

Theodora shrieked and stared dumbfounded at the slimy fish head at her feet. The queen's cry aroused Thelma and the thump of the fish head hitting the deck brought the mate running. Theodora bellowed expletives at the perpetrator. The cat, sensing the queen's volatility, kept his distance, but he was keen to glom onto the fish.

Thelma took in the scene and a feeling of dread washed over her. She'd seen poisoned fish heads used to kill wharf rats that had gotten aboard the fishing fleet when they'd been tied to the unloading docks in Maldon. She couldn't imagine why anyone would do such a thing here, but she knew she couldn't let the queen know of the deadly potential. That she-devil would love to be rid of the mate. Fortunately her majesty was far more concerned with her appearance.

"Well, if that don't make us look and smell like an old fishing scow, I don't know what would. Come on, Missy. Between the two of us we should be able to slide it out the scuppers. Can't have anyone seeing us in this state." She saw Tune-up crouched a few feet away, his tail atwitch, and hoped the queen's anger would keep him at bay.

Thelma was amazed at Theodora's determined focus when it came to her vanity. In no time the two spirits had slid the slimy mass two feet across the deck and out the scupper. It fell with a satisfying splash into the bay.

The cat eased up to the putrid goo left behind, gave it a sniff, jerked his head back and trotted back to his spot under the dodger.

The queen watched him go and gave a loud harrumph. "Fat lot of good the mate is, won't even clean the decks. I thought cats liked fish."

Thelma smiled to herself. *They do, just not poisoned fish.*

Both spirits had their compass in a spin, puzzling over the fish head. The queen took it as an attack on her vanity, whereas Thelma understood it to be an attack on the cat. But the big question for both was, why?

Matt returned late in the afternoon sporting a new pair of clear plastic sandals. They were comfortable with covered toes and a stainless buckle. He'd seen a number of Frenchmen wearing them and finally fell victim to one of the many shoe stores in town. Tune-up greeted him briefly then ran down the deck and sat next to the smear left by the fish head. Matt squatted by the mate. "What's this big guy? Whew, stinks." He looked upward thinking it might have been something dropped by a seabird from the spreaders. Noticing that the smear passed through the scuppers, he scratched the cat behind his ears. "Looks like you got rid of whatever it was. Good work."

Martinique was a big island with plenty to see and he planned to hang there for a week or two. There had been an Internet café beside the public dock so Matt repositioned *TR* until he picked up a good signal. He wanted to keep track of tropical storm activity and keep closer contact with Shanna. In her last e-mail she had asked about future sailing plans, Venezuela? Panama? The Pacific? Could it be she was thinking of more than just a visit in St. Lucia? He had mixed feelings about another shipboard companion. Since Sara's abrupt departure, he'd gotten comfortable with solo cruising, but still missed having someone to share the experience with. He wrote her back with vague plans of being in the Pacific by

November. A lot would hinge on the upcoming time they'd have in Marigot Bay.

A couple of weeks drifted by and no more fish heads landed on *TR's* decks. The tropical storm had drifted well to the north and wasn't expected to strengthen, but a new tropical depression had formed a few hundred miles east of Barbados. Matt had had his fill of bus rides exploring the steep and green and made a short move south to *Les Trois Ilets,* a calm, less noisy anchorage bordered by a couple of fancy resorts. Shanna had met her dad in Antigua and their charter would end here in ten days. He would meet them in St. Lucia.

He spent two days applying additional UV tolerant finish to the mast and boom. The queen was beside herself with the lavish attention, intoxicated by the aroma of fresh varnish. She was the only boat in the anchorage with wooden spars. Thelma silently praised her captain for his attention to detail, noting how he also gave close inspection to all her rigging, tightening loose screws and replacing fatigued hardware as needed.

Once the work was done, Matt treated himself to dinner at a French bistro that had caught his eye. Sitting alone in the open patio surrounded by potted palms and hibiscus in the tropical night, he had to admit it would be a whole lot nicer sharing this with a friend.

He had just finished his meal of seared mahi, when a tall, bearded stranger in tan cargo pants and a long sleeve white shirt approached his table and sat opposite him.

Matt was faintly amused. "Why don't you join me?"

The guy leaned forward and rested his elbows on the table. "Only for a moment, my friend."

He tensed at the voice. "René?"

"No longer. Because of you my life is very difficult now."

Unable to help himself, Matt answered in French, "*Moi?*"

"You think yourself funny, eh?"

Matt leaned in. "Dude, you are the one who made your life difficult. I was just doing my bit to keep you honest."

"Keep me honest? René laughed. "This is good."

"Did you know there was an Internet post about that dinghy the day after you stole it? If my cat hadn't shredded your arm when you tried to steal mine I may not have seen the post, but you can bet somewhere down the line you'd have been busted."

"And how is *Le Chat* from hell, hmmm?"

"He's fine, I'll pass your regards. And your dogs?"

René sat back. "With friends on land, but we sail again soon."

"You'd best head north or east, buddy, because I'm going south."

René stood abruptly and pointed a finger at Matt. "But we are not finished." Then he stalked off.

That went well. Matt paid the bill, made his way warily back to the dinghy and rowed back to the boat. "Anchor up at dawn, Mister Mate, we're bound for St. Lucia."

Chapter 39

The morning satellite shot of the Caribbean Sea showed that the tropical depression east of Barbados had evolved into a tropical storm named Bertha, packing winds over sixty miles per hour. The good news was Bertha appeared to be stationary. Matt hoped Bill and Shanna were paying close attention.

The passage to St. Lucia took nearly ten hours in light winds. Thelma couldn't have been happier and Theodora seemed to be in good spirits, especially when the captain put up the big red genoa. Even Thelma had to admit, *TR* cut a stunning wake with her matched suit of sails.

When Matt sailed into Rodney Bay on the north end of St. Lucia, he cruised along the beach until he found another unlocked wi-fi signal. Not his preferred choice of anchorages, but one born of necessity with a tropical storm in the offing. The evening satellite shot showed little change in Bertha's behavior. There was also an e-mail from Shanna saying her dad and the charter guests agreed it would be a good idea to cut the charter short a few days. If Bertha became a hurricane their guests wanted to fly out ahead of the storm. Matt was relieved and excited at the prospect of seeing Shanna in a couple of days.

Theodora was clearly disappointed. There was only one other boat in the bay and the captain dropped anchor well away from the potential admirer. Thelma watched the queen sag like a collapsed spinnaker as her ego deflated. At times like this she even felt sorry for the poor dear.

That night Bertha was upgraded to a category one hurricane, and she began to move. When Matt checked Bertha's progress in the morning he started to get a queasy feeling in his gut. The projected northwest path pretty well raked the Windward Islands. At five miles per hour it would still be a few days before he felt Bertha's approach here.

The St. Lucia website mentioned customs and immigration services were available at the Marina in Gros Ilet, only a mile from where he was anchored. He took *TR* to the visitor's jetty at 9 a.m. and was issued a cruising permit within the hour. Nobody mentioned the cat and neither did he.

Marigot Bay was known as an excellent hurricane hole and Matt, thinking lots of other cruisers were thinking the same thing, wasted no time sailing the 15 miles south. Beyond the capital, Castries, this island also became steep and green. If he hadn't been watching carefully, he could easily have sailed right past Marigot, hidden as it was in the plush foliage cascading to the sea.

There were no boats anchored in the outer harbor and the queen was voicing her displeasure. A low spit of palm-covered sand effectively blocked both the view and the ocean from the inner bay. It wasn't until Matt turned into the obscure entrance to starboard that a cluster of masts at the marina and a few boats at anchor became visible. The sight reversed Theodora's diatribe, and once again she was on parade.

Matt chose to anchor deep in the bay, but close to the barrier sand spit. He figured he could tie TR's stern off to a couple of palm trees once he had the bow anchors set. Where the spit met the hillside, a thatched balcony bar looked out over the bay. Matt rowed in with his computer and went up for a beer. The bartender, a short older guy who looked like a desiccated Santa Claus brought Matt a cold Heineken. "Nice boat."

"Thanks. Ducked in here in case hurricane Bertha shows up."

"Everyone's watching. Hoping it gives us a miss."

"You have wi-fi here?"

"Oh yeah, password is 'rumpunch', one word."

"Think anyone would mind if I tied off to the palm trees if it gets to blow?"

The guy laughed. "That's what they're there for."

"Great, but I'm with you. Hope it won't happen. When was the last time this place was hit?"

"Before I was here, but they blow through every three or four years."

Matt brought up the current outlook on Bertha and turned the screen so the bartender could see. "Looks like a category two now. Same path as this morning. What do you figure, another few days?"

"That's my bet, mate."

The next day, Bertha jumped to category three with sustained winds of 110 miles per hour. The eye wasn't all that concentrated, but storm conditions covered a hundred-mile swath. The projected path went up the east side of St. Vincent and across the south half of St. Lucia.

Matt ran two three-quarter-inch stern lines to stout palms and dove down to make sure both anchors were well set. Next, he proceeded to remove everything above deck that wasn't hardware or woodwork and stow it below. Halyards, sheet lines, mainsail, weather-cloth, and dodger all got tucked out of harm's way. Several other yachts had come in and were doing the same. The folks running the marina started moving all their boats into the mangroves at the back of the bay. When Matt had finished he rowed over and lent them a hand running spring lines and hanging fenders.

Shanella sailed in just as the first spiraling tendrils appeared in the sky. Matt spotted her under full sail entering the outer bay. He ducked below and hailed them on the VHF.

"Lookin' good, *Shanella*. Glad you made it."

Thelma and the queen were both on the spreaders watching the handsome ketch.

Theodora, unable to hand out a compliment, said, "Isn't she a pretty one?"

Ignoring Theodora's disdain, Thelma spoke more to herself. "Indeed she is. They don't get much prettier."

It wasn't until *Shanella* turned into the inner bay and Matt called out his greetings that the queen realized who it was on board. Shanna, dressed in tan shorts and light blue hoodie, stood waving from the bow. "Not her again!" she spat.

Thelma couldn't hide her delight. "Well, bless my oaken frames. We're in for a treat, Missy. You can bet the captain will keep us in ship-shape Bristol fashion as long as she's around."

As they motored past TR's bow, Bill called out, "I'm putting her bows-to in the mangroves. Can you give us a hand with the stern anchors?"

Matt hopped in Porky and in short order *Shanella* was secure in a web of nylon. When he finally stepped aboard, Shanna locked him in a tight hug that to Matt's thinking was a heartfelt embrace. He returned it in kind. "Wow, great to see you, too." He stepped back and saw lots of serious stuff in her eyes.

She dropped her gaze. "I've missed you."

"Could have fooled me."

She slugged him playfully on the shoulder. "Cad."

Bill came up and shook hands. "Thanks for the help. Glad to see you here."

Matt looked skyward to the heavy swirl of bands. "Good thing you cut the charter back. Bertha will be here in the morning."

There was worry in Bill's face. "Yeah, and it looks bad. My buddy Willis, who runs the Marina, said we could hunker down in the basement of his house for the worst of it. Sure don't want to be aboard when the palm fronds start flying." He looked wistfully around the boat. "This is her first hurricane. I hope she fares well."

They spent the next hours stripping *Shanella* to the bone. The sky turned dark before sunset.

Chapter 40

Bertha left St. Vincent in tatters and began clawing her way across the south half of St. Lucia. Reports of heavy rains and power outages preceded the big wind.

Thelma felt the first hum of wind in her rigging at midnight. It came from the south and quickly changed to shrieking gusts that tore across the sand spit blasting anything close with fine particles of sharp volcanic sand.

Both spirits were snugged into the forepeak. Matt had taken the mate and Porky ashore.

Theodora, as yet, didn't understand the threat, whining about the damage to her new varnish. It was all Thelma could do to not give her a wake-up slap.

At first it was a mild irritation up their backsides. But as the wind increased and the intermittent shrieks became a continuous scream, the burning sensation from their bums to the top of their heads grew until they were both squirming with discomfort bordering on pain.

"What's going on Thelma? What can we do?"

"There is nothing for it, Missy. We're at the mercy of the wind and I fear our lovely paint will soon be in tatters."

Then came the rain. It held down the sand and at first reduced the burn. But the sheer volume of horizontal water became like a power washer, cleansing anything remotely soft from its path.

"Thelma?" The queen held up her hand, gazing at it, mystified. Her plaintive, childlike voice caught Thelma's attention.

Thelma reached for Theodora's hand and saw instantly what was happening. Where her own hand showed with bold substance, the queen's had faded to a delicate translucence.

"I'm fading, Thelma, I'm fading." Her voice barely carried above the violence of the wind and driven rain.

Thelma, tears in her eyes, whispered to herself. "I believe it's all for the best, Missy."

She was gone in an hour. All the paint on the transom had been scoured away. Thelma was filled with bitter elation, her utter joy

174

tinged with guilt like the brackish water of the river Thames. For the moment, the hull was hers again and knowing what she knew of Theodora it was indeed for the best. But deep in the growth rings of her keel, Thelma knew there would always be a hint of the Queen, especially coming into port.

A wave slammed against her transom with a sharp jolt and brought Thelma from her grief. From the cockpit she saw another wave approach as wind and tide lashed the sea over the protection of the sandy spit. A nearby palm splintered and fell, gouging the side of a neighboring boat. The incoming wave broke over her transom filling the cockpit, her stern sank and bounced heavily on the sand bottom. Thelma felt the strain in her fastenings and the caulk in her seams compress. She couldn't tolerate much more without serious damage.

Deciding to trust in her anchors, she set to with a will, loosening one of the cleated lines that ran to a palm tree ashore. Now that she no longer shared her earthly powers with the queen her attempts bore fruit. Each time the line went slack she pulled a few inches of the tailing end from around the cleat. When at last the strain became too much the line let loose with a shot. She immediately started on the other. When the next wave hit her transom, that one popped loose and she swung out into the harbor. She watched in horror as both anchors pulled free. But as soon as they reversed direction the flukes bit deeply into the mud and sand bottom and she came up hard into the wind. Her bow now rode easily over the seas that made it past the barrier spit. Moments later a freak gust snapped one of the palms she had been tied to, falling heavily right where she'd been. It surely would have sent her to the bottom.

Around noon, as the wind and rain eased to a non-lethal level, Matt and the cat, and Shanna and Bill along with other grateful cruisers, emerged from Willis' basement and picked their way cautiously down to the bay. Oh-my-Gods, holy-shits, good-lords and other exclamations to the All Mighty were the first words out of anyone's mouth. The lush landscape had been replaced with the gray stubs of once vibrant plants. The blue water was now a sickly muddy brown. A black scar on the opposite hillside showed where a mudslide had occurred.

Matt was amazed to see *TR* anchored in the middle of the bay, seemingly untouched. His gaze drifted to *Shanella* whose bow looked buried under the root-ball of a large tree. A couple of the marina docks had come adrift and piled on one another. But there were no sunken vessels as far as Matt could tell. "Looks like we still have a home, Mister Mate."

Shaking his head, Bill's eyes were fixed on his baby. "Looks like I have a little work ahead of me."

"No, Dad, *we* have a little work ahead of us. I'm not going anywhere until *Shanella* is one hundred percent." She rested a hand on his shoulder.

Matt rowed them out to *Shanella* and as they passed *TR's* stern he did a classic double-take. "Wow, down to the bare wood."

Shanna nudged him. "Look at it as an opportunity." Then she winked.

When the hillside slid, a large mango tree had rolled over the rubble and onto *Shanella's* foredeck, snapping the forestay and smashing the bow-rail and forward lifeline stanchions. The mast, deck, hatches and bowsprit were all intact.

Bill was relieved. "Just a lot of hardware. A bit of money will fix that in no time. I think we're all in for plenty of paintbrush time."

Thinking *TR's* stern cleats had most likely been ripped out, Matt had braced himself for some serious woodwork damage. If he was lucky, maybe the lines had only parted. He was completely flummoxed to find the lines had merely come loose from the cleats. He spoke to the mate. "No way in hell did those come undone by themselves. I had a double wrap on both of them." When he retrieved the lines from the palms he saw how lucky he'd been. The fallen tree would have crushed TR's stern. The after side of the mast had been nearly stripped of varnish and for that he was grateful. His only loss was time and paint and he had plenty of both.

He'd tied Porky alongside and the lumbering spirit climbed aboard. He was anxious to see how Thelma and the queen had fared. Thelma wrapped him in a big hug. "Good to see you're still afloat my boy."

"So am I. I was really worried about a puncture for a while, all that stuff flying through the air." He looked around. "Where's her majesty?"

Thelma placed a consoling hand on his shoulder. "I'm sorry to have to tell you, but it seems we lost her in the storm. It's possible she may return, but that will be up to the captain and his good sense. So for now it's just you and me."

Porky lowered his head and looked at Thelma. "You know, I don't think she was very nice. I know she cheated at cards. Is it okay if I don't want her back?"

Thelma smiled at the boy. "I think we'll be just fine, dear."

Over the next few days, news trickled in. Power would be out in many places for at least two weeks. Mudslides to the south along with severe defoliation. Rooftops and marginal structures blown away island wide. Several deaths reported, including one lone sailor in Gros Ilet who'd had a palm frond driven through his eye.

Fortunately most of the bar was intact. A few pilings holding up the outside deck had been washed out and the thatch blown off, but a generator kept the beer cold. This was where Matt and Shanna would meet during infrequent breaks. Shanna rolled a cold beer across her forehead. "What do you think, captain? You've got a clean slate and I can do the lettering. The consulate in Castries can whip you up a Certificate of American Ownership and you're good to go." She could see he was still waffling, so she went for the kill. "Matt, the transom was blasted clean before those stern-lines came loose. That makes a good case for Thelma. She saved her own butt. Don't be letting her down."

Matt drained his beer and banged the bottle onto the bar. "Okay, let's do it."

When the road to Castries was declared passable, Willis drove his van there on marina business. Bill, Shanna and Matt rode along. During the ride, it was clear that it would be a while before the island recovered from Bertha. Besides the physical destruction, the will of the island population had taken a slam, the weight of it quite palpable. People moved as if underwater. The whole place seemed lost in a daze.

Willis dropped Matt and Shanna at the consulate, then he and Bill headed off in search of hardware. The U.S. consul shared offices with several other bureaucracies. While they waited their turn, a stern looking woman with short metallic hair, dressed in cutoff jeans and light blue work shirt came out of the French consuls office saying, "Please, Henri, talk with them. They want us to put the dogs down and I'm sure, given time we'll find a good home for them. They're both very sweet."

The consul had followed her to the door. "No promises, but I will have a word."

As the woman passed Matt and Shanna, she asked, "You wouldn't be interested in a couple of fine dogs would you? They're housebroken."

Smiling at her sales pitch, Matt said, "No, 'fraid not. We're on a sailboat."

"All the better, so were these."

Matt and Shanna exchanged a glance. "Really?" Shanna asked. "What's the story?"

The woman fluttered one hand. "Oh, the poor chap who owned the boat caught a palm frond in the eye during the hurricane. Killed him instantly, I'm told. I run the animal shelter here and the police brought the dogs to me."

Matt was afraid to ask, but did anyway. "Was the guy a tall bearded Frenchman?"

"Not sure about tall, I only saw a photo the police took. But he was definitely bearded and French."

Matt looked at Shanna. "René." Shanna buried here face in her hands.

"So you knew the fellow, did you?"

"We did, but not well."

"Well, the dogs are a problem. We'd like to keep them, but after the hurricane there are no funds available to take on any more at the shelter." She nodded toward the consul's door. "That's why I was asking the French side of it for some help, but between you and me, I reckon it's pretty hopeless."

Reaching into his backpack, Matt came out with an envelope. "Would five-hundred U.S. fix the problem?"

Shanna had a shocked look on her face, but then smiled. She remembered the e-mail Matt had sent telling her of the visit from the folks who'd lost their dinghy. "The reward!"

Tears sprang to the woman's eyes when Matt handed her the money. "You're an angel whoever you are. This is more than wonderful, such lovely animals."

Just then, the American consul called them in, so they said their goodbyes and wished the woman good luck.

The rest was simply a formality. The consul took Matt's information and told him it would probably take some time what with the hurricane relief efforts and all, but he'd leave word at the Marigot Bay Marina when all was ready.

As they left the consulate, Shanna held Matt's arm and leaned her head on his shoulder. "That was quite an amazing turn of events. Especially after your confrontation with René at the restaurant. I think I just fell in love with you."

Chapter 41

Thelma felt the familiar tickle on her bum as Shanna lettered *THELMA* on the freshly painted transom. She'd been hearing Shanna and the captain making plans for an extended cruise together. The girl definitely had what it took for the sailing life, but she'd back-winded the captain's sails when she proposed sharing the role of captain. That was a new one for Thelma as well. She'd just gotten rid of a second spirit and now she might be dealing with two captains. A boat's life was full of surprises.

Matt had taken Bill to the side after hearing Shanna's proposal. "You know she's agreed to sail the Pacific with me, right?"

"Oh, yeah, and my blessings to you both."

"She told me you guys take turns as captain. How does that work?"

"From my point of view it's great. A lot has to do with trust and I trust her with the boat. When she's the captain she takes all the responsibility. I get to relax and be crew. She develops her skills and self esteem and I get the time off to enjoy myself. It's a win-win situation. Somehow I don't think you're the kind of guy who would let his ego run the show, but if you are, you'll want to think twice about sailing with that particular woman." He gave Matt a wink. "Let's have a beer."

On a fine day in August, Matt sailed aboard *Shanella* to Martinique for the day. All her repairs had been completed. Bill was returning to pick up the boat's tender that he'd left with a friend when Bertha showed up. Shanna was the captain that day and there was no question who was boss. Matt learned first hand what a pleasure it would be for someone else to shoulder the burden once in a while. He could tell she enjoyed her role and Bill was totally at ease, happy to respond to the captain's wishes.

Back in Marigot, ensconced in Thelma's cockpit, Matt and Shanna hashed out the details surrounding her joining the boat. Tune-up was curled on her lap and they had to talk over his rumbling purr. "I'll need a month or two to wrap things up with my galleries and I have a commission to finish and deliver, but it's all workable. And just so there are no surprises, I'll be lugging along a big duffle of art supplies."

Matt gestured down the companionway. "Got loads of empty space behind the settee, so bring all you need."

"Wonderful. So how are you feeling about a co-captaincy?"

"Until today I was having my doubts, but I really liked the way you handled *Shanella*. And honestly, you're the more experienced sailor, so yeah, I'm up for it and by the sound of things, the mate is too."

Shanna reached out and squeezed Matt's forearm. "I have a good feeling about this."

He covered her hand with his. "Me, too. So where do you want to meet, Panama?"

"I've sailed most of the Caribbean with Dad, but I've never been to *Las Perlas* on the north coast of Panama, so why don't I join you in Aruba? We can make *Las Perlas* our first stop."

"Works for me. I'll get time alone with *TR*, I mean *Thelma*, and hit the rest of the island chain. Once I head west from Grenada prevailing winds should make it pretty easy to predict landfall in Aruba. I'll want to be there before you arrive."

"Watch that *TR* stuff, you might hurt *Thelma's* feelings," she said, laughing

Thelma smiled at their exchange. She had just finished a detailed inspection of her cosmetics that the captain had renewed since the big blow. There were a few spots on her varnish she thought he could have sanded to a more level surface and noticed some uneven brushstrokes on the transom. Indignation bubbled to the surface, but she caught herself. "Well, bless my pitch-pine planking. I'm acting just like the queen."

About the Author

Fritz attended the University of New Mexico, and has lead past lives as a paramedic, ski instructor and musician. He spent the '80s circumnavigating the globe in a 35 ft. classic wooden cutter. He has been a guitar maker since 1972 and is the author of four works of fiction and two of non- fiction.. He currently lives with his wife, Mari, on Washington Island, Wisconsin and Crooked Island, in the Bahamas.